ANTARCTIC ICE BEASTS

HUNTER SHEA

SEVERED PRESS
HOBART TASMANIA

ANTARCTIC ICE BEASTS

WWW.SEVEREDPRESS.COM

This novel is a work of fiction. Names, characters, places and incidents are the product of the author's imagination, or are used fictitiously. Any resemblance to actual events, locales or persons, living or dead, is purely coincidental.

ISBN: 978-1-925840-54-4

This icy dish of terror in the scariest place on Earth is dedicated to Kimberly Busse and John Kilgallon. Thank you for taking a ride to the ass end of the world with me.

THE SOUTH POLE

JUNE

AKA – WINTER OF HELL

CHAPTER ONE

The winds howled like millions of worried wolves, the walls of the base groaning and shuddering. Those walls were the only things between the winter skeleton crew and instant death by freezing. They never felt as paper thin as they did right now.

Dallas Kazmir stared at the cards in his hand but couldn't concentrate.

"You want we should switch to Go Fish?" Chris Rodriguez – C-Rod to everyone at the base – asked irritably. He'd been the hot hand for once and he was anxious to keep the streak rolling.

Dallas chucked two cards into the center of the table, not caring what he'd given away or drew. His eyes darted to the ceiling, the hanging overhead light swaying uncomfortably. A hard gust shook the floor. The stack of poker chips in front of C-Rod collapsed.

"This is ridiculous," Holli Sorensen said before raising the pot. "How long did Jean say this storm would last?"

Swallowing hard and dry, Dallas replied, "Couple days." Just hearing it said out loud made his stomach churn.

C-Rod chuckled. "Dude, you're whiter than my Irish girlfriend's ass. You need to go see North and get one of his special chill pills before you shit yourself."

The snow pelted the base like fastballs.

"Lay off him," Holli said, concern etched on her face. Dallas was the veteran of the maintenance crew. This was his fourth winter and he'd seen it all. If this storm had him tenser than a piano wire, they should all be worried.

"I'm just kidding," C-Rod said, taking a swig from his beer.

"You should take it easy with that," Dallas said to him.

"Why?"

"Because you might need a clear head. Storm like this, anything can happen at any time."

The Freedom Base was the only permanent base on the South Pole, built five years after a massive storm destroyed the original Amundsen-Scott South Pole Station. Thirty-seven people had died that winter, their bodies, and the demolished station, not found until September when the sun rose and the weather made it possible to fly a recovery crew in. Not all of the bodies had been recovered. Eight were missing, presumably dragged off by predators, never to be seen again.

Construction on the Freedom Base began several years later, engineers working tirelessly to anticipate even the worst storm so there would not be a repeat of the tragedy. Freedom Base was built on an ice sheet at an elevation of over nine-thousand-three-hundred feet. The raised facility was designed specifically to withstand everything nature could throw at it. It was, as Dallas had said many a time, a brick shit house series of connected structures. Long and boxy, they were nothing much to look at. *Better Homes and Gardens* wouldn't be knocking on their door anytime soon. Their form and function were perfectly suited to the harsh environment.

A night like tonight – night being relative, since they were going to be in darkness for the next several months – Dallas couldn't stop thinking about the remains of the Amundsen-Scott Station and its inhabitants. The twisted wreck and pale, petrified bodies had been removed, but their spectral presence remained. At least they did in Dallas' mind.

"Call," Holli said, trying to take his mind off the gale force winds.

Dallas threw down his cards and got up.

"Read 'em and weep," C-Rod shouted, sweeping poker chips his way.

Walking across the room, Dallas went to the bulletin board where they posted each day's to-do list and put his palm flat against the wall. It was as if he and the base had become one, the violence of the storm flowing into his bloodstream, riding his central nervous system and flooding his brain with images of slashing white fury.

"You're only winning because we don't give a shit," Holli said. "Besides, you're so deep in debt to us, you're still working this season for free."

"Few more nights like this, maybe not, Hols." He shuffled the cards and called out to Dallas, "Hey Texas, I'm not done with you yet."

It'll hold, Dallas thought over and over, a mantra against his rising fear.

"I think we're done, buddy," Holli said, rising from her chair and heading for the coffee maker.

"Sore losers," C-Rod muttered.

It'll hold.

It'll hold.

"We should walk the base, make sure everything's okay," Dallas said to the wall.

During a storm like this, it was best to do hourly interior checks to make sure there were no cracks in the structure. If the biting winds found even a pinhole, the temperature would plummet and turn anyone nearby into a popsicle. Snow driven with unrelenting power would rush through the gap and pile up with alarming speed. With everyone else asleep – though Dallas suspected most had to pop a pill to get some shut-eye – it was important that he and his crew watch over them and make sure they would wake up alive and well in what passed for morning here.

They were, all of them, nothing more than glorified caretakers. Freedom Base needed someone to help it survive the long, dark winter. What little science occurred during the season was of minor consequence. A lot of money went into building the compound. These four, shuddering walls were worth more in the eyes of the US government than the seven lost souls sent to live within them. Only misfits, outliers, would willfully choose to winter down here. They were expendable. Dallas had served ten years in the Marines. He knew all about expendable.

"We can pick up where we left off after," C-Rod said.

"Or not," Holli replied, taking a long sip of coffee.

"Whatever. I got a couple of zombie flicks I wanna watch, anyway."

"You and your zombies. Why do you waste your time?"

"It's better than chick flicks, I'll tell you that. Why don't you come cuddle with me one day and we can watch one together, show you how much fun they are."

"In your dreams, creepo," she said with a smirk. "Now, do what Dallas said."

Dallas removed his hand from the wall and turned to her, appreciative that she was on his side, but upset with himself for causing the flickering of apprehension in her eyes. He had to get his shit together. "Let's go. And take your time. No rush jobs tonight."

Holli nodded, heading off to her assigned sector. C-Rod flicked the bill of his Cubs baseball cap and moseyed out of the rec room.

Taking a deep breath, Dallas put his hands on his hips and looked around at the mess they'd made. There was popcorn on the floor, magazines tossed all over the couch, and a pile of sawdust on the shuffleboard table from when Hols went to sprinkle more and the cap fell off. If not for the howling storm, it was the picture of normalcy.

But there was no ignoring what was going on outside. Dallas had paid his dues in Antarctica and had lived through more squalls than he could count during his travels around the world in the military and as a civilian. This one was different. It felt to him as if it was sentient, its ire focused on Freedom Base and the vulnerable, weak humans inside.

"Stop making yourself crazy," he muttered.

He was about to head over to the science lab when the floor began to rumble.

CHAPTER TWO

"Did you feel that?"

Jeannie Nichols sat up in bed, instantly awake. Her husband snored beside her. She jabbed him with an elbow and slipped out of their bed.

"What the hell, Jean?" Rob said, rubbing his eyes.

She was in the corner of the room struggling into her pants. As if on cue, the room shook, a pair of paperbacks tipping off the shelf above the computer table and thumping to the floor.

That woke him up. Rob looked about the room. "Where are my clothes?"

Jeannie was tucking her shirt into her pants and donning a cap to cover the mass of red, bed head curls. "I don't know. Wherever you left them. Meet me in seismology when you find them."

Without waiting for a reply, Jeannie burst out of the room, running down the darkened, narrow corridor to the base's science pod. She stopped dead in her tracks when the overwhelming cacophony of what sounded like a dozen freight trains colliding filled the air. It was so loud, for a moment she irrationally thought the power of the sound waves alone would be enough to shatter the reinforced walls.

"What the fuck?"

The terrifying noise stopped. Her heart went into overdrive. Jeannie waited, expecting to feel the slight vibration of an aftershock through the soles of her booted feet. What she did feel was the pounding of footsteps coming up behind her.

"You okay?" Earl Sherman said as he pulled up alongside her. He was still in his boxers and sweatshirt.

"I was until I heard that."

Sherm attempted a feeble smile. "It almost made my dreads stand on end."

Having Sherm with her broke Jeannie's paralysis. Together, they ran the rest of the way to the science pod. Dallas was already there, ashen-faced.

"Please tell me that was nothing," the head of maintenance said.

"I can if you don't mind being lied to," Sherm replied, settling in front of a row of monitors that were never turned off.

Jeannie took the chair behind him and logged into her computer. The base had gone mercifully still. Even the wind had died down. The room was alive with the sound of clacking keys. "What do you got, Sherm?"

He exhaled loudly. "Not as bad as it sounded. Only a 5.9 on the scale."

It was funny, or not so funny being that they were in the literal middle of nowhere with no way to get help should they need it, that Sherm had talked about the *sound* of the earthquake and not the rocking and rolling. Jeannie had been present for dozens of earthquakes and had never, ever heard anything like that. She looked to Dallas, who was standing by the door with his eyes popping out of his head. "You should meet up with Rob and do a full assessment."

Dallas shook his head and his eyes went back to where they belonged. "Yeah. Yeah, you're right." He buzzed Rob on the walkie. "Nichols, where you at?"

Her husband's tinny voice responded quickly. "I'm in the kitchen now. Everything looks all right. Meet me in storage."

"Be there in a few."

Dallas hustled out of the science pod.

The storage room. Jeannie knew that the initial compromise of the Amundsen-Scott base had been in one of their storage rooms. It was nothing but chaos, destruction and death after that.

She opened a dozen programs spitting out a slew of flashing numbers, rising and falling bars, alerts and reams of data. Her eyes ran across the screens, her brain on fire, taking everything in and mapping out what was going on beneath them.

Just think, she was in bed not five minutes ago dreaming about a simple summer barbecue with friends in the yard.

The wind returned, knocking to be let in.

There'd be no barbecues down here.

Two hours later, everyone was gathered in the science pod. Normally, team meetings were held in the rec room, but it seemed appropriate to be in the one place that could provide answers.

Since there were only seven of them here for the winter, there was plenty of room for everyone. Rob Nichols drank from his mug of coffee, the black X-Files mug a gift from his sister many moons ago (underneath the logo, it said '*The brew is in here*', waiting for the nervous chatter to die down.

Seven people.

The previous station would typically be staffed with up to forty men and women, hunkering down for months of endless glacial night. Both the Amundsen-Scott and Freedom Bases were run by the USAP (United States Antarctic Program) under the auspices of the National Science Foundation. When the Amundsen-Scott Station had been destroyed, the USAP decided to make the next station smaller, more compact and able to weather any kind of storm. Nichols knew that another riding factor behind shrinking the size of the base was to limit the potential death toll should something go wrong. Seven people dying in a place and season where only crazy people dared tread was far more palatable than three or four dozen. There was bad publicity and *bad* publicity. Nichols often compared them to the early astronauts – men (and now women) taking incredible risks, knowing their lives were at stake, but fostering just enough invincibility to still think death was something that happened to other people.

We're all a little bit broken in our own ways, Nichols thought. Rational people with stable lives would never entertain a winter on the Pole. It was no shock to him that several of the crew had brought black Misfits t-shirts. The eighties punk band certainly embodied the spirit of those who dared to winter at the Pole.

The crew was a tad excitable at the moment, but there wasn't an air of dread hanging over the room. Well, maybe not Dallas. The guy looked completely wigged out. He wasn't joining in any conversations, just staring at the walls and ceiling every time the base was hammered by a gust of wind. The earthquake may have passed, but the storm was still raging, and would be raging, for another day or more.

"So, what's the deal?" Rob asked his wife and Sherm, the only scientists signed on for the winter. During the summer and spring seasons, the eggheads far outnumbered the grunts. Now, with darkness and killing frost, most of the science was about recording weather patterns and seismology, the two very things his wife and Sherm were experts at.

"Looks like the worst of it is over," Sherm said, his long arms folded behind his head. His fingers played with one of his dreads. "The aftershocks have died down to the point where we can't even feel them."

Exhaling, Rob said, "Good. We got through the worst of it with no structural damage. Though I am sorry to report, Hols, that your old school McDonald's glass didn't survive the fall from the kitchen counter."

Holli made a sad face. "Oh no, not Grimace!"

"You want a glass with a purple blob, or to be alive?" Dallas said.

"I was just kidding," Holli replied.

Dallas looked away.

C-Rod patted the maintenance chief on the shoulder. "You need to take it down a notch, Texas. Crisis is over."

"Get your fucking hand off me." Dallas stepped away from him. "And unless you're deaf, dumb and blind, the crisis is not over."

"What, you're now the earthquake whisperer?" C-Rod joked. No one laughed with him.

The room shook a bit, but not from an aftershock.

Dallas pointed at the ceiling. "You think that's not a crisis? Tell me, what's the color of the sky in your world?"

Rob looked to his wife. This was their first winter down at the end of the world. He looked to Dallas as their resident expert and if the man was worried, well, that was nothing to shrug off.

"Jean, what about the storm? We still have another day to go?"

Rob's wife glanced at Dallas and looked like she wanted to slink out of the room. "Yes. It's going to sit on top of us for a few more hours, then slowly move on to the west. But…"

If there was one thing Rob didn't like, it was buts.

Biting her lip, Jean said, "It looks like there's another storm right behind it. And that one is worse. The predictive systems are saying we could be facing seventy mile an hour winds or more."

The continent of Antarctica was known for its high, punishing winds, some reaching to almost two hundred miles an hour. But because of the topography of the South Pole, that region rarely saw anything over fifty. At least until the storm that ripped the Amundsen-Scott Base to shreds. At least that's what the recovery team assumed.

"Jesus," C-Rod said, dropping into a chair. "My mother's house got wrecked by Sandy when it hit Jersey, and the winds were the same."

"Good thing this isn't your mother's house," Terry North, the facility's sawbones, said. North was over fifty, a widower and two-time cancer survivor who proclaimed to have given up the fear game years ago. He could be a bit of a know-it-all, but he did stay cool as a well digger's ass under pressure.

"Cut the smug act. This is some serious shit," C-Rod spat, pointing a warning finger at North.

"Put that finger away before you hurt yourself," North said, smiling.

Rob Nichols jumped in before things escalated. The last thing he needed was a brawl in the science lab. The equipment was expensive as hell.

"What's the size of it?" he asked Jeannie.

"Um, I guess massive would be the best way to describe it. Oh, and growing."

Dallas abruptly left the room.

Adjusting his cap and tugging on his beard, Rob shook his head. "How is it we didn't see it until now?"

"It must have formed while we were sleeping."

"Something that big just popped up out of nowhere?"

"I don't know what to tell you. It wasn't there four hours ago, and now it is."

Holli rolled her eyes. "Sure, climate change doesn't exist."

North countered with, "The question really isn't whether climate change is real or not. The planet is in a constant state of shifting climate patterns. What puts a bug up everyone's ass is the old blame game. As self-hating humans, it makes us feel better to hold ourselves responsible because it gives us hope we can patch up the boo-boo and make it all better. Truth is, the Earth doesn't need us to alter the weather. It and the sun do just fine all by themselves, and when they decide it's time to mix things up, there's nothing we can do about it. If we face that fact, we feel helpless and weak and no one can step in and make a lot of money off the misguided intentions and fear mongering that man made it and can un-make it."

With her hands on her hips, Holli said, "How did you get so cynical?"

"Being a realist isn't cynical. Just like being young and dumb isn't a crime."

"You're not making any friends here," Nichols interjected.

North looked around the room and chuckled. "Guess I'm not. That's what happens when my beauty sleep is interrupted."

"Okay, the earthquake is in the rearview mirror, right?"

"From everything I'm seeing, yes," Sherm said.

"And this current storm is going to start dying out, correct?"

"Yes," Jeannie said.

"No damage to the station?"

Holli and C-Rod shook their heads.

"And we're all up and walking and talking, so that's all good," Rob said. "I say we call it a night and get back to what we were doing. In my case, it was drooling on my pillow. Any objections?"

When there were none, he called the meeting adjourned.

Everyone but Sherm shuffled out of the science pod. "I won't be able to go back to sleep without keeping an eye on things for a while."

"It's a free country," Rob said.

"I don't know what the hell this country is, but it sure doesn't feel free," Sherm replied, his face glowing blue from the monitors.

Nichols thought he was right at that. From now until September, they were basically prisoners in here. He slipped his arm over Jeannie's shoulders and they walked back to their room. She looked up and down the now empty hallway and said, "I'm still concerned about the sound that quake made."

"Why? Even you just said the quake is responsible for it. It's like being afraid of thunder."

She looked at him as if he were the densest man alive. Compared to her brilliant brain, he just might be, but he'd happily resigned himself to that when he said 'I do.'

"Thunder is air. That was the wail and cry of the Earth itself adjusting. God knows what the physical after-effects could be. It would be great to look around, but we can't, not with this and the next storm beating the daylights out of us."

They stepped into their dark room, the automatic lights flickering to life a few seconds later. Rob kissed her and pulled her in for a hug. "Our job is to make sure the scientific instruments, the base, and everyone in it remains in working order through the winter. When the sun comes up in a few months, we can explore and see if there are any changes to the surface. But until then, you're stuck with me, our off-kilter crew and your curiosity. Okay?"

She patted his rump. "Not really, but it'll have to do. You want a melatonin?"

He dropped his clothes beside a chair, slipping into the bed in his boxers and undershirt. "Unlike Dallas, I kinda like the sounds of the storm. Is it weird that I find it soothing?"

"With Dallas looking like he just saw a ghost, yes, it is weird. But I didn't marry you because you were normal. What other man would come down here with his wife?"

Jeannie took off all of her clothes, tossing her bra on his face.

It didn't take a genius to know what they would be doing for the next fifteen minutes, or more if he were up to it.

CHAPTER THREE

Dallas could end his shift in another hour, but with the way his nerves were jangling, there was no way he could even think of sleeping. The steady hammering of the storm was like a stick poking him every time he got the slightest bit drowsy.

And that earthquake didn't help matters much. It was only the second shaker he'd experienced at the Pole, and though he was grateful it hadn't damaged the base, the eerie sounds it made still rang in his ears.

Walking the hallway of the resident section, he muttered aloud, "Keep it together, man. Everything's good. We're all warm and safe."

But for how long? Another even bigger storm was headed their way. And from what he knew about earthquakes, the aftershocks could come much later and be worse than the initial shake, rattle and roll. Sherm said everything looked good for now, but that could change in a New York minute.

He turned the corner for the enclosed walkway that connected the resident hub with the common areas. He'd do another inspection of the kitchen, rec room and storage room just to be safe.

Knowing his unsettled demeanor was getting to the others, he'd sent Hols and C-Rod to their quarters, assuring them he had everything covered. By the time the rest of the crew was ready to start their day, he'd be heading off to bed where he could keep his wild concerns to himself. Sure, there was a heck of a lot going on outside in the bitter darkness around them, but that was a day in the life of the South Pole.

So why was he so freaked out?

His grandmother, God rest her soul, used to tell him he was born with a caul, an ancient sign that he was brought into this world with the special gift of 'sight'. He'd yet to see into the future. If he really had the gift, he'd have picked the winning lottery numbers by now. Grandma had been a bit of a fruit loop, making pancakes in the shape of witch faces and jack-o-lanterns in the morning for him and reading Tarot cards for her friends and neighbors at night. She would have been right at home in some little cottage in the forest in a Grimm Brothers fairy tale.

Dallas hoped to hell and back that his so-called gift wasn't kicking in now. He just couldn't shake the feeling that something was wrong.

Maybe, back in his room, he'd knock back a couple of shots of Dewar's he kept under his bed and try to zone out to old episodes of *All in the Family*. A comedy was definitely needed to lighten his mood.

The kitchen was just as fine as it had been when he'd been here an hour ago. He opened the fridge and grabbed a bottle of water and some cheese. With the water in his pocket, he munched on the block of pepper jack and flicked on the lights to the storage room. It was crammed with food and other essentials, with boxes on racks that went up to the ceiling. They'd be here for over five months, and they had stocked up for seven just in case. You could never be too cautious. It didn't take much for something to go wrong and things to go tits up.

There you go again.

If this had been his first tour in the Antarctic winter, he'd write this off as first time jitters. Or the beginning of cracking under the isolation and constant realization that help, should anything go wrong, was not on the way. Even an infected toe from clipping your nails too short could kill you down here.

He made his way to the science pod. Sherm was gone, hopefully catching a few minutes of shuteye. Dallas looked at the monitors but couldn't understand a single thing on them. Nothing was glowing red or flashing DANGER, so he had to take that as a good sign.

His stomach balked at the cheese and he tossed the remains in the garbage, rinsing his mouth with water. The walls rattled a bit when the wind kicked up, but all was well.

All but Dallas.

Maybe he would ask North for a pill. That and the Dewar's should set him right. Maybe he was just tired. He hadn't been sleeping all that well lately. Too many dreams about Paula, the woman he'd met a month before coming down here. She was a hell-cat in sheep's clothing with legs that went on forever. They'd met in a farmer's market, her flimsy prairie dress revealing a lot of her sumptuous curves. It took four dates over the course of two weeks before he got to see those curves up close and personal. That left them two weeks of intense getting to know you time. Now he was gone for months and she was free to meet any man who came along. She promised she'd wait, but could he really expect her to sit around for him when they'd essentially just met?

"A man without problems is a dead man," he said, heading to the rec room. A single, low wattage light lit the room. It had been tidied up, most likely by Hols. C-Rod was a slob who left a trail of garbage in his wake.

There was a lone window in the wall by the bookshelves, the thick pane of glass revealing darkness blacker than tar. Dallas pressed his nose against the glass. The snow may have been swirling but he couldn't see a thing. He flicked the wall switch to turn on the outside lights.

A pale, hairless man was caught in the harsh glare. He looked at Dallas with large, almost black eyes, before darting out of the arc of light and into the pitch.

Dallas stumbled backward, hitting the ping pong table and knocking it over. His mouth opened in a scream but no sound escaped.

Someone was out there! Someone that didn't look quite right.

And he hadn't been wearing any clothes.

CHAPTER FOUR

Rob Nichols sat on two stacked crates in the storage room, Dallas sitting opposite him. It was cold in the room, their breath mingling in the space between them like dancing snakes.

"You feeling better?"

Dallas knocked back his fourth shot of vodka, part of Nichols' private stash. When he'd first knocked on his door, Nichols thought Dallas was there to tell him part of the base had been breached. His near-heart failure was replaced by perplexity, and now concern, as Dallas told and retold the story of the naked man outside their door.

"Not really," Dallas said.

They'd been in here an hour. Nichols wanted to keep this away from the rest of the crew. If the vodka didn't settle him down and his story didn't change, it was likely he was having a break, which meant they were in trouble. The man knew every nook and cranny of Freedom Base. If he had to be put out of commission, that would leave Nichols, a first timer, to pick up the slack.

"Did you at least check for footprints?" Dallas asked.

"I looked outside and didn't see any," Nichols replied. "But with the way the snow's coming down, any prints would be buried in minutes. Now, what makes you think this guy was naked?"

Dallas raised a bushy eyebrow. "Because he didn't have any clothes on."

Nichols shook his head. "No, that's not what I'm asking. You and I both know, if we were to step out that door, naked as a pair of jaybirds, we'd be dead before we could say, 'Oops, I forgot my coat!' You understand why I'm finding this hard to believe, right?"

Dallas abruptly stood up, tossing the shot glass across the room. "I'm not making this up! I saw him."

"Did you see what he was doing?" Nichols decided to let it play out. Maybe if he asked enough questions, Dallas would start to realize how ridiculous and impossible all of this was sounding.

Scratching at the stubble on his cheeks, Dallas said, "I think he was trying to look inside the rec room. Like, maybe he was seeing if it was empty."

"And why do you think he'd do that?"

"Hell if I know. Maybe he wanted to break in, but not if someone was around to see and hear him. Maybe he wanted to catch Hols leaning over the sink so he could look down her shirt. I…don't…know."

"All right, all right. Who knows what goes on in anyone's mind, right? Now, you said there was something off about his eyes."

Wagging a finger at him, Dallas said, "No, I told you his eyes weren't even human. They were big. Like twice as big as anyone's eyes should be. And they were black."

"There's lots of people with oversized dark brown eyes."

"Uh-uh. Not like this. His eyes…they had no whites. There were all black, like an animal's. His ears, I think they were pointed. And he had no hair. Not a fucking whisker or eyelash. He was balder than a newborn baby. Except he wasn't no baby. He was big, like me, only muscular."

"And naked," Nichols said, feeling like his plan had failed.

"And naked."

Now Nichols got up. He capped the vodka bottle. Dallas had had enough. "This is a hell of a lot to lay on me."

Dallas grunted. "Yeah, just think how I feel. I had to see the freak."

But did you? Nichols thought but dared not say. "You know who I want us both to talk to next."

The big man deflated. "I know. He's just gonna stick me with a needle to calm me down, put me to sleep and say everything will make sense in the morning. I can tell you, ain't nothing going to make sense to me ever again. No. Not after this."

Nichols clapped him on the back. "Come on, buddy. Might as well get this over with."

As they left the storage room, Nichols saw Holli heading for her quarters. Her eyes lingered on Dallas and it was impossible not to notice the recognition that something was up on her face.

"Heading off to bed?" Nichols asked.

Her smile couldn't be faker. "A nice, hot shower first. I'm beat. You two up to no good?"

"As always," Rob said, chuckling.

"Well, not much trouble to get into in this place. See you later."

Nichols silently thanked her for not prying.

He and Dallas went the other direction, toward the medical unit.

"So?"

Nichols had been pacing outside the door like an expectant father. After he'd left Dallas in North's care, he'd run over to tell Jeannie he was dealing with something but not to worry. By the look on her face when he left, he'd accomplished the exact opposite.

Terry North was a burly man with a black handlebar mustache and longish hair tied into a ponytail. He looked more like a biker than a doctor, but that was all part of his 'I don't give a shit anymore' look on life. North cracked his neck and sighed. "That's one hell of a story, I'll give him that."

"Is it the start of cabin fever?"

It seemed hard to believe Dallas could ever experience cabin fever, especially at this juncture of the winter season, but anything was possible.

"Could be," North replied.

"Or…"

"Or a lot of other things. He told me he hasn't been sleeping well lately. He left behind a new honey and the distance between them is working on his mind, especially at night when there isn't anything else to do but choke the chicken, ruminate or sleep. I gave him a sedative and asked him to sack out here so I can keep an eye on him." North rummaged around his pocket and retrieved a pack of gum. He offered a stick to Nichols, who declined. "He's not fighting me, which tells me he's very aware that protesting too much will make him seem crazy. So, he's either rational and conscious of his actions and reactions, or he's gone off the deep end but is clever enough not to appear bat shit."

Nichols couldn't help himself from laughing. "Bat shit? They teach you that in medical school?"

"Hell, they didn't teach me anything about the human mind other than how to dissect a brain. I passed on psych classes because I didn't want to get into people's heads *that* way." He blew a small bubble that popped quickly. "Big Texas is going to be out for a while. I'll check in on him from time to time."

"I hope he wakes up and realizes he was only dreaming."

"You forgot one more thing," North said.

"What's that?" Nichols asked.

The doctor opened the door and looked in at the slumbering man. "In a world where reality stars become presidents, maybe Dallas is telling the truth."

Nichols stared at North, a quiet game of chicken, waiting for the man to smile or laugh or do something to chuck that statement off as a joke.

When he didn't, Nichols simply turned and walked away, wondering if insanity was contagious.

CHAPTER FIVE

Jeannie and Sherm spent the day shift, which was as dark and foreboding outside as the night shift, glued to their computers. She'd been worried about what her husband was up to earlier, but the work kept her mind busy and occupied.

Sherm had printed a map of the South Pole and tacked it to the wall. It showed the Freedom Base as a small dot, that dot surrounded by undulating wave patterns. Not far from that dot was a large, red dot, denoting the epicenter of the earthquake. It had been so close to the base, less than two miles, that it was a miracle they were still in one piece. The close proximity may explain the strange sound, as they were in the lone front row seat to one of the planet's deadliest dances.

"All quiet on the southern front?" Jeannie asked, pinching the bridge of her nose and looking away from her monitor. To combat eye fatigue, she made it a point to focus on the blank ceiling for one minute every twenty minutes of screen time. She'd read somewhere that it helped, but today, the niggling headache at her temples wasn't making things better.

"Praise Jesus, yes," Sherm replied. "If I had wood nearby, I'd knock on it and say we should be good from here on out."

"Religious and superstitious. Interesting," Jeannie joked.

"I'll be whatever I have to be to make it out of this endless freezer from hell. How's that storm coming?"

"Oh, it's coming."

Faster and bigger than I first thought.

"Well, the hatches are already battened, so I guess all we can do is wait," Sherm said. He was so focused on another earthquake popping up that the severity of the storm didn't enter his full consciousness.

The storm had her full attention. The winds now could top eighty-five miles an hour and seemed to be climbing as it picked up in intensity instead of petering out as it moved further inland. It made no sense. If it kept up at this pace, all hands were going to have to strap themselves in and pray Freedom Base didn't fly away to Oz.

When her walkie chirped, Jeannie jumped, knocking over her cup of coffee. Fortunately, it landed on the floor rather than the equipment.

"Jean Genie," Rob squawked. He'd been calling her that after the David Bowie song since their second date when they'd watched *Labyrinth* together.

"I was wondering if you have a lunch date."

Jeannie smiled. "I have had a lot of offers."

"Ah, but I'll bet none as good as soup and grilled cheese in our, hmm, utilitarian kitchen."

"You had me at utilitarian. I'll be right there."

"Roger that, Blue Jean."

Her stomach rumbled, the thought of food making it aware just how empty it was. Jeannie had skipped breakfast, her concern about the storm and earthquake overriding her need to start the day out right.

Not that there was day. Not here. Not for months.

She tapped Sherm on the shoulder. "You heard the man. I'll be back in a bit."

"You think you could bring me back a bowl of SpaghettiOs?"

"I can't believe you still eat that crap. You know it was specifically designed to appeal to the immature taste buds of children under ten."

Sherm flashed his bright, even teeth. "If you don't feed the child within, you start to grow old. That's not gonna happen to me."

Jeannie wagged a finger at him as she left. "You keep feeding the child in you and you'll get sick, just like us old folks."

Before she left the science pod, she looked at the bank of surveillance monitors arranged outside the base. Most of them were pointed at the base itself so they could see any damage or areas that needed snow removal without having to go outside to check. Others looked away at the vast expanse of pitch black nothing. If she were back home in Chicago, it might be windy but the sun would be out and a nice walk down Michigan Avenue for some window shopping and lunch at an outdoor café would be an atypical day for her but she'd take it in a second.

Some days at the Pole, days like today, the seemingly never-ending space around them felt more like a physical presence, a fist of oppression tightening over them bit by bit. She realized just how trapped she was in here, the weight of isolation pressing down on her chest until it was hard to breathe. She closed her eyes for a moment and put her hand on her chest.

Thank God she had Rob.

At least he could make her laugh or put things in perspective. He was the perfect sounding board for her fears, giving back warm comfort and protection. He didn't know it yet, but she planned to reward him for going on this mission with her to what was essentially a foreign planet. They may have been married, but they'd yet to settle down, Jeannie's wanderlust an unstoppable force. Rob, who had seen combat and endured her trips to Alaska for dogsledding; Africa to not hunt but get as close to possible to wild, savage game; and even bungee jumping off the side of a helicopter hovering over Niagara Falls, wanted a more sedentary life. More than anything, he wanted them to have a child, to settle down and grow old. He no longer asked her about it, which to her meant he'd given up. As torn as she was, her desires for their future pulling her in many directions, it was time for her to think of Rob. And their future boy. Or girl.

First, they had to get out of this damned place. What she thought was going to be an adventure was really endless monotony. Even the storm and earthquake couldn't ignite the thrill seeker within her. She lived on danger, but now that she too wanted to start a family, she wanted more than anything else to be safe and secure. She was anything but that down here.

Jeannie chased the feeling of desolation away with thoughts of his smile (even though it was under the beard he insisted he grow on this trip) and crisp, buttery, gooey grilled cheese.

Rob Nichols heated the flat top grill, staring out the window into the black. He'd turned on the outside lights, the glow reflecting off the snow and making it look something like daylight. The faux lunchtime view was a nice touch, but if he was being honest with himself, there was a small part of him hoping to catch a glimpse of Dallas' strange looking naked man.

If anyone was out there with no clothes, they're deader than Michael Jackson by now, he thought.

Now, if Dallas had seen a man dressed in protective gear, Nichols would have been gathering his team to head outside and find him. They were a good distance from any of the other scientific outposts in Antarctica, but it could have been possible for someone in a Sno-Cat or specially designed Humvee to get here. The odds were slim, but that made more sense than some naked man walking about as if he were at a nude beach. Most of the other stations were at the coast, Freedom Base being the only one at the South Pole itself. If something had gone catastrophically wrong at one of them, a lone survivor could have set out, gotten lost in the driving snow, and ended up here.

Though with the temperature hovering around minus-fifty, it was hard to believe anyone could have made it this far.

"Dammit, Dallas, now you're making *me* crazy."

He was coating the flat top with butter when his wife's voice floated into the room. "You know, talking to yourself is the first sign that there be trouble ahead. Especially when you're talking to Dallas, who from my vantage point, isn't here."

Nichols loaded one of the sandwiches on his spatula, four kinds of cheese between two slices of white bread, and slipped it onto the flat top. "Some of the greatest thinkers in history regularly talked out loud to themselves."

She kissed the back of his neck. "I don't think anyone's going to confuse you with a great thinker any time soon."

He turned to her, spatula upraised, tempted to tap her nose and smear it with butter. "You know you should never insult the man in charge of cooking your food, right?"

"I'll take my chances." She went to the fridge, grabbed a bottle of some blue sports drink, twisted the cap and leaned against the prep counter. "So what's going on with Dallas? He was spooked by something before."

That was when he was just getting antsy about the storm.

There was no way to keep a secret in a place this small, especially when there were only a handful of them huddled inside. Nichols added the second sandwich, stirred the pot of lentil soup and turned to Jeannie. "Dallas is in sick bay sleeping off a sedative North gave him."

"Should we be concerned?"

"I don't know."

Jeannie took a sip from her alien looking drink. "This next storm is going to pound us like chicken cutlets. He'll be a mess over that one."

Nichols hesitated.

She knew him better than he knew himself. "What are you not telling me?"

"He saw someone," Nichols said, turning away from her questioning gaze to flip the sandwiches.

"He saw someone? Where? It's not like we're open for guests."

He pointed out the window.

"That's not possible," Jeannie said.

"I agree, which is why he's sleeping now with North watching over him. But that's not the crazy part."

"I'm almost afraid to ask."

"The guy he saw, Dallas swears he was naked."

Jeannie's bottom lip was grabbed between her teeth. He hoped she wouldn't bite so hard she'd draw blood. Whenever she was worried, her lip paid the price for her nervous energy.

"There's more," he said.

"I can't imagine."

"No, you can't. He said the man was completely hairless, not even eyebrows. And his eyes were huge, like an owl's only bigger, and totally black."

"Oh, honey, that is so not good." She looked crestfallen. Everyone loved Dallas. They counted on him to get them through the winter. Maybe this was the 'one trip too many' for the big guy. Looking at it that way, Nichols would prefer a strange man prowling the base to Dallas losing it.

"Tell me about it. Can you pass me those?" He plated the grilled cheese sandwiches, cutting them diagonally so the cheese ran out like lava. After ladling soup into a pair of bowls, they sat down to eat. Neither touched their food.

"Is there a chance he did see someone out there? Maybe the light and snow distorted his view of the guy." Jeannie picked up a triangle and let it hover between her plate and mouth.

Nichols sighed. "I sincerely doubt it."

"Where did he see this weird man?"

"Outside the storage window."

She finally took a bite, deep in thought. Nichols dipped his sandwich in his soup.

"Camera four catches a part of that area. We can go back and check the file."

Jeannie was just like him, hoping Dallas was, in a way, right, and not going stir crazy.

"Okay, but after we eat," he said.

They chewed in silence for a while, until Jeannie looked outside and said, "If there was someone out there, all we're going to find is a snow covered body."

And guilt, Nichols thought, over not believing Dallas and getting his ass outside to do a thorough perimeter check. The food sat in his gut like lead as he realized he was fucked either way.

CHAPTER SIX

Dr. Terry North peeked in to see Dallas still slumbering, his snores almost louder than the storm that had finally moved on. He checked his watch, an old Mickey Mouse timepiece his mother had given him when he turned nine. He'd found it in an old storage box in his attic when he was preparing to ship out to the Pole. His mother had long passed – breast cancer took her from him when he was in college. His frustration with her doctors made him switch from economics to pre-med – but wearing the old watch made it feel as if she were here with him.

He was hoping the maintenance man would be awake soon. North wanted to sit and talk over coffee.

Dallas had seen something. No matter how crazy his story sounded, there was nothing in the man's eyes that betrayed even a glimmer of doubt. North had worked in Bellevue Hospital in New York for two years and had been around his share of delusionals and total nut bars. Dallas was neither.

"What did you see?" North whispered.

Nichols wasn't buying it, and who could blame him. A naked man in the sun under the best temperatures down here wouldn't have long to live.

North thought, in that respect, Dallas was somehow mistaken. The man he saw could have been wearing some sort of environmentally protective outfit that simply made it look like he was nude, thanks to bad lighting and anything on the glass that smudged Dallas' view.

It was the eyes that bothered North.

Of course, that could be the same misinterpretation. But when Dallas talked about the eyes, he transitioned to a man who would forever be haunted by what he saw.

North was the oldest member of the team and had seen three times more shit than any of them thanks to a life well lived. For a man of science, he had a very open mind. There was the year he and his now deceased wife spent living in what she swore – and he was hard pressed to deny – was a haunted house. The sounds of a child laughing, the patter of feet up and down the stairs at night, the soft touches on their legs, made him realize there was more to this world than meets the eye. It gave him hope that the patients he'd watched die were moving on to, if not a better place, at least not oblivion.

The only thing impossible in this world was the concept that there was an impossible.

Knotted with concern, North went to his office, sat and waited.

Holli Sorensen woke up two hours after she'd hit the sack and was wide awake. She tried for an hour to reclaim the dream she'd been having about playing kickball with her friends in the old neighborhood, but it just wasn't happening.

She knew the risks coming down here, but the earthquake in tandem with a coming storm that had Jean raising an eyebrow, unsettled her.

Picking up a book about a modern day hermit living in the Maine woods, Holli read not to get drowsy, but to take her mind off of Dallas. Truth be told, the way Dallas had behaved was what unmoored her the most. This was her first time and she'd been told Dallas was one of the most experienced men in all of Antarctica.

And now he was worried, which meant she should probably be shitting herself.

Holli put down the book and grabbed her phone. She scrolled until she found the one remaining picture of her ex, Nigel. He was wearing the suit he'd bought for his cousin's wedding, his smile bordering on his infectious laugh. He was so handsome, she remembered staring at him in his sleep and wondering how she'd ever landed such a perfect catch.

Except there was no such thing as perfect, as she discovered when she found Nigel between the spread-eagle legs of her friend, Gillie.

"It's your fucking fault if I die down here," she said.

She was tempted to text him just that. If something tragic did happen, why should he get to live his life guilt free?

But no, that was petty. Holli may have been mad, but she was never petty.

What was petty about death?

C-Rod had popped a sleeping pill and chugged a beer before getting into bed. He'd never told anyone at the base that he had claustrophobia. It wasn't a problem while he was busy working or shooting the shit with people. That took his mind off things. But when his shift was over and he was in his room, that coffin-feeling pressed in on him bit by bit.

Thank God for pills and porn.

He snored now, a trail of drool from his cheek to his dampening pillow, the grunts and groans still playing on his laptop that had slipped off his lap and now sat at a precarious angle on the edge of his bed. He dreamt of nothing, just the way he liked it.

Nichols checked on Sherm while Jeannie went to pull the file from the camera four feed on her laptop in the rec room.

"You need any coffee?" Nichols asked.

Sherm, who had been dozing, popped his head up. "Huh?"

"Hold on."

Nichols popped a cup in the coffee machine, a minute later bringing the steaming cup to Sherm. "Tall, sweet and black, just the way you like 'em."

Sherm accepted the cup with a wistful smile. "Hell, they can be short, bitter and orange right about now. You don't know how lucky you got it."

Nichols laughed. "Oh, I know. And if I start to forget, Jeannie reminds me. How's everything going outside?"

"Silent and not deadly, just the way I like it. That doesn't mean we're in the clear, but I'll keep watch just in case."

In case of what? Nichols thought. It's not like they had anywhere to go if the mother of all earthquakes was about to hit them. He wasn't sure he wanted to know in advance that he was about to be swallowed into the earth. Better to live in ignorance.

"Okay. I'll return your partner to you in a bit." Nichols knocked on the doorframe and went to the rec room. The silence of the station was eerie. The storm had passed, half the crew was asleep, the other half working quietly.

It was the literal quiet before the storm.

Jeannie was on the couch, tapping away at her keyboard.

"You got it?" Nichols asked.

"Yep. I'll throw it up onto the big monitor."

There was a fifty-inch monitor on the wall opposite them. Most of the time, it was used for watching movies, the crew killing time watching a lot of comedies. Down here where real life was scary, they needed the levity. *Superbad, Bridesmaids* and *The Forty Year Old Virgin* had been in steady rotation.

Nichols settled beside his wife and watched the screen. The video was stark white with pitch-black on the outside border. The outdoor light bounced off the snow on the ground, creating a near white out. It wouldn't have been so bad on a small screen, but the cutting starkness of it made them both shut their eyes.

"You should have warned me," Nichols said.

"Yeah, well, I hurt us both, so there."

Snow zigzagged in diagonal sheets. There was nothing to see. Not even a stray penguin.

"I rewound it to the time of the tremor," Jeannie said. "I saved you a lot of shaky cam, since I know how much you love it."

She never let him live down the time he puked in his popcorn bucket when they saw *The Blair Witch Project* on the big screen. He wasn't a fan of found footage movies because of the way the cameras jerkily moved, nor did he enjoy going to the IMAX theater.

He kissed her cheek. "Thanks, babe."

"You want me to fast forward until we see something?"

"Not too fast. I don't want to miss anything. *If* there's anything to see."

`He prayed there was something. The alternative meant Dallas had lost it.

Forwarding at the slowest speed possible, Jeannie and Nichols stared at the monitor. The time between the quake and Dallas swearing he saw something – no, *someone* – was only about an hour and a half.

It would have been impossible to tell the image was moving faster than real time if not for the speed of the falling snow. It reminded Nichols of watching silent movies, people and objects moving at a kind of warp speed that made everything seem funny.

He was about to ask Jeannie to pause it to give his eyes a rest when he saw something and shouted, "Stop right there!"

Jeannie's hand flew to her mouth. "Oh my God."

Frozen on the monitor was the image of a man walking into the frame. He was tall and muscular and horrifyingly naked. His back was to them, bulging muscles taught in the sub zero temperatures.

What Dallas had forgotten to mention was that the man's flesh was almost whiter than the snow.

Nichols had the immediate urge to run for the head.

"Now," he said breathlessly, "let's take it one frame at a time."

The man stared off into the unknown black for what felt like an eternity. Nichols found himself chanting, "Turn around, you son of a bitch. Turn around."

Dallas was also right in that there wasn't a hair on the man's body, though he could have had light blonde hair that wasn't being picked up by the camera. But his head was shaved, his ear jutting from his skull as if his momma may have had some bat in her lineage.

"Here he comes," Jeannie said, biting on a nail. Her finger hovered over the key to pause the video. For now, it silently ticked away, the head turning their way inch by agonizing inch.

Jeannie yelped when his face came fully into view. She pushed the laptop off her legs as if it were a giant spider. Nichols grabbed it before it hit the floor and stopped the video.

"Holy shit."

It was as if the strange bald man with the biggest, blackest eyes were staring at them, *through* them. His mouth was shut in a grim line, his nose wide and flat against his stark face.

Jeannie regained her composure. "Is…is he deformed or something? I mean, how can a person have eyes like that?"

Nichols stared into those depthless orbs, wondering how deep they'd have to dig in the snow to find the body. Would those eyes in death remain so obsidian, as alien and foreboding as they looked at this moment, captured by a camera twelve hours earlier?

"If there's anyone who would know that, it'll be North. Sit tight and I'll get him."

Jeannie got up and turned off the monitor. "I don't mind staying here, but I can't stare at…him."

CHAPTER SEVEN

Nichols did something he'd never done before. He locked the rec room door.

He, Jeannie and a bleary-eyed North watched the video of the bizarre, impossible man over and over again. Once the man stepped into view, he looked into the camera for a few moments, his face devoid of expression, and moved on, back into the black nightmare from which he'd come.

"I'll be a son of *The Weekly World News*," North finally said, pinching the bridge of his nose and getting a cup of coffee.

"What?" Nichols said. He was perched on a chair in a catcher's squat, fighting the nervous energy that demanded to be released.

"Either of you remember *The Weekly World News*? It was a rag you'd find by the cash register in supermarkets."

"Sure I do," Jeannie said. "My mother would buy one every now and then and me and my sister would read the crazy articles. President Clinton had a love child with an alien. Bigfoot was spotted in the New York sewers. Nazis were running a secret lab off America's east coast and making monsters. Crazy stuff."

North gave a slow nod. "Exactly. I got a kick out of that paper, though I always wondered if there was anyone who actually believed the insanity it cranked out. You must remember the most famous cover model in the paper's history?"

Jeannie's face lit up and she pointed at the man on the monitor. "Bat Boy! Holy Christ, he looked like Bat Boy all grown up!"

"What the heck are you two going on about?" Nichols said.

"I weep for the hole in your youth," North said. "Google it later." Turning to Jeannie, he said, "Unfortunately, our Bat Boy, or should we call him Bat Man, is very real and I will assume, at this moment very dead. I suggest we go out and find him."

Frustrated, Nichols said, "We all know that isn't a bat man. I wanted you here to tell me what could be medically wrong with him."

North walked up to the monitor and stared at the frozen image. "Hard to tell from a video. Not to mention the image isn't the best, what with the snow acting as a very poor filter."

"What about his eyes?"

The eyes bothered Nichols the most. He was sure that's what unhinged Dallas, too. Naked in the snow could happen. If someone had gotten lost outside from one of the other bases, hypothermia could make people mistake that they were burning hot and they would remove all of their clothing.

Tapping the screen with a pen, North said, "Well, the size could be due to several things, like hyperthyroidism or Graves' disease."

"What can make an eye all black like that?" Jeannie said. Her arms were wrapped around her torso as if she were trying to give herself a bear hug.

"He could have been high as a kite. The camera lens may not be giving us the truest image. Or he could have been hurt, and what we're mistaking for big, black eyes is actually blood. That's the one I'm putting my money on. Again, we need to find his body."

The door clicked and Nichols jumped from his chair.

Dallas stood in the doorway, a key ring in his hand.

"So no one thinks I'm crazy anymore?"

"I never thought you were crazy," Nichols said.

"You did. And I don't blame you. I was kinda worried that I was losing it." Dallas looked at the wall monitor and closed the door. "Weird looking son of a bitch."

"I'm going out to look for his body while we have a break between storms," Nichols said. "You in?"

Dallas popped his knuckles nervously. "Yeah. He couldn't have gotten far. I'll get some shovels."

North had wanted to go, too, but Nichols didn't want to risk it. He was the only doctor they had and any trip outside was dangerous, even if it was just to take a few steps out the door.

Naturally, Jeannie wanted in as well.

"I'll feel better knowing you're safe inside," he said.

"You know that's sexist, right? Leave the woman behind while the men go hunting?"

"No. It's a husband who loves his wife and doesn't see the need for her to risk her life. You don't like it, take it up with HR."

He didn't give her an opportunity to talk circles around him and make him change his mind. She'd done it many times before, and in this case, his word was final. "Dallas, let's go suit up."

The two men went to the prep room that contained their protective gear. Dallas had procured a pair of shovels and nylon rope. "What's the rope for?"

"When we find him, we'll have to drag him inside. He'll be frozen solid. Might be hard to carry."

Nichols went and got a small sled and tied the rope to it. "I don't want to damage the body any more than we have to."

They suited up, layer after layer. Nichols slipped into his insulated overalls, followed by a down jacket, balaclava, wool hat, headlamp, gloves and final layer, the standard issue thick, red coat everyone called Big Red. It was insulated and big enough to accommodate all of the layers underneath. Plus, it was bright, which was crucial. You did not want to get lost out there.

No matter how many layers they put on, that first gust of frigid air went straight to their marrow. Nichols took a deep breath and steadied himself. It was around minus-eighty, cold enough to make you see stars.

Mercifully, there was no wind, but the darkness at the edge of the base gave him another reason to shiver. Guidelines had been set up around the buildings so people didn't get lost. He and Dallas clipped themselves onto the guideline, Nichols in the lead. The snow cracked like ice beneath their heavy boots. Only a couple of inches had accumulated from the previous storm. Contrary to popular opinion, the South Pole was not bombarded by constant snowstorms. It was actually pretty dry, too dry for much precipitation. However, howling winds scooped up existing snow and scattered it to new portions of the pole.

Those same winds raked the snow, obliterating any footprints or tracks.

Nichols and Dallas made their way to the wall outside the storage room, where the naked Bat Man had been spotted.

"You see anything?" Nichols asked. His headlamp and the extra flashlight he'd brought swept the bare ground.

"Nothing," Dallas said. "Not that I expected to. Let's keep going. He went that way. I'm sure we'll find him close by."

Nichols stared into the black. He tied a rope onto the guideline and headed into the nothingness. Dallas stayed close behind him.

"Why couldn't he have stayed close to the buildings?" Dallas grumbled.

There were three buildings in Freedom Base, though only one was occupied in winter. The others housed all sorts of science equipment and living quarters for the summer shift. They'd been shut down for the winter, though each had to be checked on daily to make sure the elements hadn't found their way inside.

"I still want to know where the hell he came from," Nichols said, his breath practically turning to ice the second it wafted through his balaclava.

Dallas looked around. They were miles and miles from the nearest living person, naked or otherwise. Somewhere out there had to be an abandoned vehicle. "Maybe he dropped from the sky. The wind was pretty bad. Kinda like when it rains toads on one town because a tornado scooped them all out of their ponds from another several miles away."

Stopping and turning to him, Nichols said, "Are you messing with me?"

Dallas shook his head. "Saw it on the History Channel."

"The channel that has all those shows about us coming from aliens? Oh, then it has to be right."

They trudged on, their crunching footsteps the only sound in the southern desert. Nichols was hyper aware of the moment when they stepped out of the confines of the floodlights and into the vast nothing. He looked back at the base, as if to make sure it was still there, the lone haven in this never ending emptiness. He didn't like straying this far. Not here where it was easy to get turned around and lost…and dead.

With their flashlights and headlamps trained on the ground, they searched for any odd lump or shape. The Bat Man should have collapsed somewhere right around here. There was no way he could have survived much further. Not in this cold and without clothes.

A tug of guilt prickled at the back of his skull.

I should have listened to Dallas.

At the very least, I should have checked the camera right away.

Now a man, no matter how odd he seemed, was dead because of him.

No, the second he walked out here without clothes, he was already dead.

That gave Nichols little comfort.

"Where the hell is he?" Dallas grumbled.

"Maybe he walked back home. Wherever that is."

Before they'd left, Nichols had asked Jeannie to put out a call to the other bases to make sure no one was missing. He and Dallas were the only search and recovery team that were going to be out here until the summer season. He was sure when they got back inside, they'd have the identity of their man. He just hoped they'd have his body to send home, too.

Dallas adjusted the intensity of his lantern, putting it up as high as it would go. The harsh light did its best to battle the darkness, illuminating nothing but pure, white snow.

"Nothing." Dallas pulled his balaclava down and spat, the liquid turning to ice before it hit the powder.

"That's impossible. Let's go this way."

Trudging to their left, Nichols checked the rope. They were running out. There was no way in hell they would get to the end and even walk two feet without it. That would be suicide. There was no need for three stiffs out here.

Nichols' jacket was getting heavier. It felt and sounded like it was starting to freeze. They were running out of time. The warmth and safety of the base was calling.

"I don't think he's here," Dallas said when they came to the end of the line and started following the rope back.

"He must have the stamina of a polar bear to get any further from here. Come on. We can try again later with more rope and widen the search. It's not like his life is in the balance. Let's warm up. I need an Irish coffee."

Dallas patted his shoulder. "Make that two."

Nichols was in the process of turning around when the beam from his flashlight caught something paler than the snow.

He stopped.

It was a pair of legs.

Standing upright.

He reached behind him and tugged on Dallas' coat.

"What?"

Nichols pointed.

There was more than one pair of legs.

His light inched upward, slowly.

Five men, all naked, hairless and with the same large, black eyes as the man on the video stood still as statues. Their arms were slack, hanging at their sides. Their bodies sparkled in the light, encased in pinprick crystals of ice.

"Are they dead?" Dallas whispered. A sudden breeze carried his query into the ether.

"I don't even know if they're real," Nichols said. They looked to him like a display of statues. They all looked the same. He couldn't detect a single difference in any of their features.

They had to be some kind of statue. Was another outpost playing a gag on them? The statues could have been placed out here at the very tail end of summer, just before night fell.

But how would that account for the man they caught walking around the base?

Dallas said, “I’ll be damned if I know –”

One of the statues blinked.

Then another. And right on down the line.

When their mouths opened in unison, a deep wail emanating from their bizarre, cookie cutter faces, Nichols and Dallas ran.

CHAPTER EIGHT

Dallas slammed and locked the door, his back against it, trying hard to catch his breath. His lungs stung from the cold.

Nichols ripped his hood, hat and balaclava off and tossed them in a corner. Neither spoke a word, but the look in their eyes said plenty. Once they settled down, Nichols hunched over with his hands on his knees, Dallas asked, "What in blue hell are those things?"

Yes, he'd said *things*. They may have looked like men, but they certainly weren't.

"I don't have a fucking clue."

"For all we know, there are more of them out there."

Nichols didn't answer, but Dallas could see the man's jaw working. The question was, what did they do now? It wasn't as if there was a contingency plan for coming across naked humanoids who made sounds no human throat could replicate.

"We have to tell everyone," Nichols said, stripping down to his clothes. "Get Hols and C-Rod. I'll grab Sherm, North and Jeannie and we'll meet in the rec room. You know what to bring."

Dallas was glad Nichols had been with him this time. That and the video they'd captured would at least keep anyone from doubting him.

Suddenly, he wished he *were* crazy.

As they hustled into the corridor, Dallas said, "What do you think they're doing out there?"

Nichols shrugged. "One thing they're not doing is freezing to death." He ran toward the science pod, his heavy footsteps stomping away from Dallas.

Pounding on the door, Dallas shouted, "C-Rod, I need you in the rec room, now!"

When there was no reply, he knocked harder. "C-Rod! Leave your wet dreams behind and get out here pronto."

There was a thump at the door. C-Rod had thrown a boot or something heavy. "I'm coming, man. Chill out."

Chill out. Dallas didn't think he'd ever be able to chill out again.

Before he could knock on Holli's door, it opened and she stepped into the corridor. She was already dressed, her red tresses tucked under a cap.

"What's going on?" She didn't look like she'd just woken up.

"We'll discuss it in the rec room," he said, hustling past her to his own room. Nearly knocking his door off its hinges, he lunged at his locker, finding the metal box on the top shelf. Using a key on his key ring, he unlocked the box and palmed the lone key inside. Next, he ran to what they called the office. This is where Rob Nichols filed his reports and spoke to their bosses. It wasn't much to look at, just big enough to accommodate a desk and two chairs, but it did contain something very important Dallas hoped they'd never have to use.

Opening the bottom drawer, he pushed aside a stack of manila folders. Underneath was a false bottom with a small lock. He used the key he'd extracted from his locker and opened it.

The loaded Glock 217 was exactly where it had been placed originally, never having seen the light of day…until now. The .45 caliber weapon held thirteen rounds and had efficient and deadly stopping power. Dallas had hoped to never see the damn thing. Almost all stations in Antarctica were weapons-free. He could only think of one station run by the Germans that had a rifle on hand.

When Freedom Base had been constructed, it had been decided that it would contain one firearm in case of emergency. With no police or military presence on the continent, there was no help coming in a crisis. A crisis down here would more times than most mean having to subdue someone who had simply gone mad. It had happened before. Dallas remembered a man at the United Kingdom Edmund Post who had suddenly and without warning started speaking in tongues. Rising from his spot at the dining table, he'd proceeded to lift his chair and smash everything he could get his hands on. People around him had said his eyes had practically rolled to the top of his skull as he babbled in increasing volume, destroying the mess hall. At first, he was given wide berth, the startled scientists unsure what to do. Once their paralysis broke, it took six men to take him down, one man having his arm snapped in two. It had been winter at the time, and the insane scientist, who until that day had been a father figure to many of the younger staff, had to be locked in his quarters.

He never did regain his senses. For months, people lived in fear that he would escape, his manic cries keeping them awake, turning them all into shuffling zombies.

Dallas suspected that the higher ups at the USAP considered that someone from the destroyed Amundsen-Scott Base had flipped their lid, sabotaging it and leading to one-hundred percent fatalities. Hence, the gun.

He never, ever wanted to have to use it on his fellow crew members, not even when C-Rod spent entire days intentionally getting on his nerves.

But those things out there? He wouldn't hesitate to shoot.

The second Jeannie saw her husband, she knew something had gone wrong.

"Where's Sherm?" he asked, his chest rising and falling rapidly.

"I think he went to the restroom." She got up from her chair and gripped his upper arms. "What happened out there?"

He leaned in close to whisper. "We found…we found other men."

Jeannie gasped. "Are they hurt? Did they say where they're from? Where are they now?"

Rob shook his head. "They're still out there. There's five of them and they're identical to the man we saw on the monitor." He licked his lips, his parched throat clicking. "I don't know what they are. The sound they made. Christ, I can still hear it in my head."

She had never seen him like this before. Rob was given command of Freedom Base both because of his military background running similar outposts around the globe and his exceedingly calm demeanor. In a place like Antarctica where tensions and fear ran high, a steady hand at the wheel was an absolute necessity.

Rob looked terrified.

And it rocked Jeannie to her core.

"Hey guys," Sherm said, tying a band around his dreads to keep them in a long, ropy line down his back. "If you want to make out, I can come back later."

Jeannie hadn't realized how close she and Rob had gotten, her eyes searching his own, their arms on one another. Making out was the last thing on their minds.

"We have an emergency meeting in the rec room," Rob said, working hard to keep his tone neutral.

"Emergency? Is the storm getting worse?" Sherm said.

"I want to tell everyone at the same time. Come on."

Rob broke away from Jeannie, striding toward the rec room. She hurried after him, wondering if she should also bring up that the incoming storm's intensity had increased and that they were in for one hell of a wallop.

CHAPTER NINE

Rob Nichols stood before what he realized, not for the first time, was a team too small to be left to fend off the winter. If there were more of those strange men outside, they were going to be grossly outnumbered. A chill ran through his body. He shook it off. Everyone looked concerned, Dallas standing at the back of the room and staring out the window. Even C-Rod wasn't wearing his usual doofy grin.

He was the fist to speak up. "What's going on, Nichols? Is there a breach somewhere? Just point me and I'll fix it."

Nichols waved him off. "No. No breach." He took a deep breath. "Look, I'm not going to beat around the bush because that's a waste of time. Dallas and I went outside because a man was spotted walking around the base."

"A man? How can that be?" Holli asked. "It's not like you can just take the wrong bus and end up at the South Pole."

"I'm not sure what he is," Nichols said before anyone could chime in. "Not only that, Dallas and I encountered five of them. They all look exactly the same, and they weren't wearing a stitch of clothing."

Now C-Rod chuckled. "Naked dudes in the South Pole? Yeah, right."

Nichols motioned for Jeannie to pull up the image on the monitor. When the pale, nude, bat-like man came into focus, the sound of chairs scraping against the floor filled the room. Everyone but North leapt to their feet.

"What the fuck is wrong with him?" C-Rod said. "And how is he standing? He should be face down in the snow."

Sherm cautiously approached the monitor. He turned to Nichols and asked, "You say there are four more just like him…out there?" He pointed to the wall. All heads swiveled to the window, the brightly lit snow mercifully devoid of the alien men.

"At least four more," Nichols said. "They were staying just at the edge of the lights, waiting in the darkness. There could be more. I don't know and I don't think any of us wants to go out there fumbling in the dark looking for them."

That was something on which they all could agree.

Holli clutched the bill of her cap as if she were fighting the wind to keep it on her head. "This doesn't make sense. It's not even possible."

"It doesn't and it is," Dallas chimed in.

"How are they even alive?" Holli asked, looking to North.

The doctor sucked on his teeth, deep in thought. "I wish I knew. Nichols, are you sure you saw five of them, all identical? Maybe it was a reflection from the ice."

"Trust me, there were five. I thought at first they were statues, not that statues appearing out of nowhere makes much sense. When they saw us, they opened their mouths and started to – well, not exactly scream, but they made a sound that was as inhuman as they look. That's when Dallas and I hightailed it back in here. Luckily, they didn't follow."

North said, "Could be the light hurts their eyes. With pupils that large, it would feel like getting their skulls pierced by a lance."

"The one on the video doesn't look bothered by it," Jeannie said. He just appeared, to her, to be scouting the base, perhaps looking for a way in. She wrapped her arms around herself.

North nodded. "That's true."

"Maybe we should go outside and fuck them up," C-Rod said. "I don't like the idea of someone or something that looks like that hanging around."

"Genius plan," Holli scoffed. "And what do you do if there's ten of them, or more? You going to be able to punch your way through them?"

C-Rod made a fist, admiring it. "I've been through worse."

"Worse? Look at him! You come across anything like that in the big, bad streets of Framingham?" Holli got in C-Rod's face.

"Settle down," Nichols said, his voice leaving no room for argument. "No one is going outside. Right now, we're the ones in the safest place."

"Maybe they'll just freeze to death," Sherm said. "What is the temperature headed down to?"

Jeannie said, "We're looking at minus one-fifteen. Maybe colder by this time tomorrow."

"No way they could survive that," Holli said.

"I don't know," Dallas said. "They seem to be doing just fine now."

"A lot of wind coming with it," Jeannie added. "If they don't freeze solid, they'll get blown away."

"It would be a shame not to get our hands on at least one of them before that happens," North said.

Dallas stared at him incredulously. "You want one? Be my guest and go get one. I'm sure they'll be happy to come inside for a hot bowl of soup and a blankie."

"I'm just saying, in terms of medical science, they're a wonder. Their bodies have perfectly adapted for an environment of extreme cold and darkness. If we could find out how, it could change not just polar exploration, but how we approach even space travel."

C-Rod stalked to the coffee machine and poured a cup. "I think you're in fucking space, doc. I wouldn't want that in here, even if it was dead."

Jeannie's heart fluttered. "Speaking of which, do we have anything to defend ourselves with, just in case?" The deadliest weapons she could think of were some broom handles and ping pong paddles. Well, that and maybe Dallas' meatloaf. But they wouldn't have time for food poisoning to take effect if those men outside attacked them.

Dallas reached into his pocket and showed them the Glock. "We do have this, which is more than any other base down here."

"One gun?" C-Rod said.

"Hopefully one gun is more than we need," Nichols interjected. "For now, I just want everyone to be on the lookout. We'll break up to man windows and the camera monitors. Once the storm comes, we won't be able to see anything anyway."

"And we can hope that our worries fly off somewhere over the rainbow," Sherm said. "Or at least far enough away to never find Freedom Base again, especially in the dark."

Rob asked Jeannie to stay with him, but she refused. Everyone else had to be on their post alone and she should be no different. She stayed close to the science pod, darting between it and the rec room to check on the incoming storm. They had about four more hours until it hit. No matter what those men out there were, she couldn't see them surviving the storm. Not out there, unprotected without even a stitch of clothing.

The image of that man-thing made her stomach cramp. It terrified her. The view outside the rec room window was barren as always, but he/it could be just a few feet away, enshrouded in darkness, staring in at her at this very moment.

"What the hell are you?" she whispered, her breath fogging the glass.

Jeannie Nichols had never been a shrinking violet. Growing up a tomboy and a daredevil, there were very few things that scared her. Of course, that intimidated all of the boys, which made it hard for her to get that elusive first date. Rumors of her being a lesbian irked her but she daren't lash out because she didn't want to then be branded homophobic. All of that changed when she met Rob in her junior year in college. He liked to claim that he'd tamed the wild beast, but look where they were now. Living in the dark hell of the South Pole winter had been her idea, her passion, for years. While Rob had his reservations, she was ready to jump on the plane the moment she got the acceptance letter to be the base's climatologist for the winter.

She'd been so excited. Compared to this, bungee jumping was as thrilling and death defying as jumping rope.

Was that a shadow encroaching along the wedge of light?

Jeannie stared, unblinking, until her eyes hurt.

It must have been the wind shifting the powdery snow.

For the first time in her life, Jeannie was scared. She wanted Rob beside her more than anything in this world. But she couldn't give in to her fear. None of them could. If they did, it could mean death for them all.

Dallas kept to the main entrance. His palm sweat coated the Glock's black grip.

As much as his initial shock at seeing that man outside had rattled him, he was inclined to agree with C-Rod. Better to take the fight to them, if indeed a fight was even necessary, than sit in here cowering like frightened children. His gut was telling him to sit tight, but his heart screamed for him to suit up and go out there with C-Rod, Nichols and Sherm. That bit of rekindled fire helped restore his balance. He'd never been so off-kilter before. It was like how certain animals behaved strangely before an earthquake. And there *had* been an earthquake immediately following Dallas' moment of weakness.

What he wouldn't give for his Adirondack chair, a cooler of beer and a warm day of clear, blue skies.

Living down here was not his ideal, but it paid extremely well. He'd been doing six months on and six months off, his free half-years spent lazing about and doing anything he wanted, for years. Maybe it was time to get off the Polar Express. This was a young man's game and the days of his youth were well past him.

The one benefit to his stints at the Pole was the cessation of his nightmares. He didn't know why they refused to plague him when he was on the icy continent and he didn't question it. He was just grateful that working in no man's land saved him, albeit temporarily, from the memories of that horrible day in Fallujah. Christ, what a fuck-up. He'd been forced to see a military shrink both while he was in and out of the service, but it did no good. Neither did drinking or sleeping pills. The only cure was Antarctica. Maybe because in the bitter cold, his mind couldn't reach far enough to drag him back into the oppressive heat of an Iraqi summer.

He keyed his walkie talkie. "Hols, how's everything looking?"

Holli was sitting behind the bank of monitors showing the outside camera feeds. She would most likely be the first person to see anything strange approaching.

"All clear," she said.

"Everything still working?"

"Cameras are getting a little shaky from the wind, but they're up and running."

"Good. How about you, C-Rod?"

There was a pause, and then his tinny voice replied, "Nada." C-Rod was in the kitchen, looking out at the rear of the base.

"Sherm?"

Nothing.

"Sherm, you read me?"

A crackle of static, then, "Sorry. I had to drain the lizard. I don't see anything but snow."

Nichols piped in. "Before you ask, there's nothing much going on here." Nichols had opted to keep looking out the windows of the living quarters in a constant rotation from room to room. "Just the way I want it."

A gust of wind howled, rattling the station. Dallas looked to the ceiling as if he could see into the angry face of the rapidly approaching storm. His mouth hung open, the walkie temporarily forgotten.

"How about you, Dallas?" Nichols said.

Dallas shook his head to clear his mind and tapped the mic button. "Nothing out here but wind, ice and snow."

He looked down at the gun. Nichols had stationed him here because it was the central and easiest access point to the station. Better the man with the gun defend their weakest link.

"I have a pristine view from my perch," North reported. Dallas didn't appreciate his flippant tone. This was as serious as a cancer diagnosis. He decided not to reply to him lest he said something they'd both regret.

"How about you, Jeannie?" he said.

"Clear," she replied in a clipped tone. He wondered what worried her more, the men outside or the storm above.

Dallas reached into his shirt pocket and pulled out a single stick of beef jerky. He put the gun down on a shelf to unwrap the snack, his mouth watering at the first salty bite. He wasn't hungry, but he knew he had to keep up his strength, just in case. Chewing on the jerky, he kept his eyes peeled on the small, square pane of glass in the upper center of the door. Chewing on the jerky also helped to keep his senses alert. It would be too easy to be dulled by the boredom of staring at unchanging scenery, even with the thought of being surrounded by unknown beings. He knew full well from his countless hours on sentry duty, waiting for death to come at any second.

He was about to go for a second stick when Holli broke the silence.

"Holy crap, I see them!"

CHAPTER TEN

"Where? How many?" Nichols said.

Dallas dropped the jerky and picked up the gun, squinting into the light and dark.

The time it took Holli to reply felt like eons. "Eleven. No, fourteen. Wait, there are more coming."

"They're over here!" C-Rod shouted so loud it was almost impossible to understand him. "I see them!"

"Dallas, I want you to stay put," Nichols said. "You spot any of them by the door, let us know."

"Roger that," Dallas said. With the base constructed on a multi-level raised platform, the kitchen area was the highest from the frozen ground. Those man-things wouldn't be able to get up to the window. There were, however, steps to the door where he was stationed. If they were making their move, he assumed they'd find their way here. He wished to hell more ammunition had been provided. He'd just have to make every shot count.

"I'll cover the door with Dallas," North said.

Dallas took a deep breath, listening to the chatter on the walkie, and waited for the inevitable.

Nichols ran as fast as he could, getting to Holli before Sherm and Jeannie.

Holli pointed at the monitor filled with the identical men. There were more than fourteen now. Nichols estimated there had to be at least a couple dozen. They strode through the ankle high snow in an odd, jerky unison, their black eyes open wide and staring.

"What are we gonna do?" Holli said.

Nichols stared over her shoulder at the monitor. "We're going to watch them, for now."

Jeannie and Sherm ran into the room, followed by C-Rod, who knocked over a narrow rack holding boxes of spare electronic parts. "What the fuck?" he said.

The naked men were carbon copies of one another. They suddenly stopped their march, their faces turned upward toward the camera.

"They know we can see them," Jeannie said. She nestled close to Rob. He could practically feel the electric charge of fear coming off her, which unsettled him even further. He put his arm around her waist.

"What are they doing?" Holli said. She gripped an iron bar she'd found earlier.

"I don't have a clue," Nichols said. "Sherm, I need you to get a distress call out now."

"What do I say?"

"Tell them we have a few dozen men surrounding the base with what appears to be ill intentions. Do not mention what they look like. If you do, they'll just think you've flipped your lid."

"Gotcha." Sherm darted out of the room.

Nichols knew that there was no way help was going to come. What he needed to do was have a record of what was happening here, even if the full truth was not revealed. If they ended up like the previous base, at least their deaths wouldn't be an entire mystery.

Was this what happened to the Amundsen-Scott Base? That entire compound had been utterly demolished. Perhaps it was by the hands of those things and not a freak storm.

He could tell the wind was picking up by the speed and slant of the driving snow being picked up from the ground. The men stood motionless, unaffected. They didn't even blink. How was that possible?

"If they're waiting for an invitation, they can go scratch," C-Rod said.

"Maybe they're trying to figure out a way to get inside," Holli said.

Despite their otherworldly appearance, Nichols detected an intelligence within them. They would know how to get in. This was all some kind of show.

A few of them staggered, finally breaking their tightly held ranks, as the wind rocked them.

"North was definitely wrong about the light hurting their eyes," Jeannie said. "Which makes me think that black isn't all pupil. Their entire eyes must be solid black."

"One thing they ain't got is shrinkage," C-Rod said. Each man was well-endowed, and from what Nichols could see, the length of the appendage was the same for each being as well. He couldn't spot a single difference between any of them. As crazy as it sounded, he was beginning to think of them as creatures not of this planet. How could they possibly be terrestrial? The Earth was a system of chaos, producing no two things alike, even among identical twins. There was always a difference.

No, these…people looked like something produced from a lab.

"Jesus," he said.

"What?" Jeannie said.

"You think they're some kind of experiment that got out?"

The South Pole's residents were mostly scientists. Though studies like climatology and geology comprised the bulk of the research down here, another nation could very well be developing high-tech cloning far away from prying eyes. Antarctica was actually the perfect place to engage in activities that best remained secret and hidden.

"You think there's some Frankenstein around?" C-Rod asked.

"You have a better explanation?" Nichols said.

"Yeah. I'm still asleep and this is all a freaking nightmare."

Sherm bounded into the room, panting. "Radio communication is out."

Nichols gritted his teeth. It wasn't a shock, not with the storm coming their way. Or maybe one of those things had taken out the communication tower. He pulled up the video feed for the tower. It was clear of the pale men and still standing. "Of course it is," he grumbled.

"Wait. Look," Holli exclaimed.

The bat men snapped their heads in the same direction, looking over their right shoulder. It was a quick, simple act, but it made Nichols' skin quiver and his spine alight with sharp prickles.

Like a flock of birds, the men ran.

Nichols grabbed his walkie, "Dallas! North! They're coming your way!"

"How many incoming?" Dallas asked.

"Too many. I'll be right there." He tapped C-Rod. "Come with me. The rest of you stay here. Keep trying the radio and keep watching those monitors. If these fuckers break up, I want to know where they're headed."

Jeannie tugged on his sleeve and the look in her eyes nearly melted his resolve. "We can't let them in," she said gravely.

"I know." He kissed her hard and cupped her cheek.

Armed with only a butcher's knife he'd taken from the kitchen, Nichols and C-Rod ran to the entrance. Nichols wondered if he'd ever see Jeannie again.

Racing down the narrow corridor, both men nearly lost their footing when something struck the base with the fury and power of the hammer of God.

CHAPTER ELEVEN

Dr. North watched the mob of black-eyed men barrel toward them. Dallas' face was pressed close to his as they peered out of the window set in the door.

"Fuck me sideways," Dallas muttered.

North was having a hard time catching his breath. How on Earth were they supposed to hold the door with one gun and a mop handle?

He grabbed Dallas by the arm and pulled. "Back away from the door!"

The men hit the stairs, launching their bodies against the door with reckless abandon.

Wha-whump! Wha-whump!

The door shook but held. Hell, the entire building was rocked.

"Quick," Dallas barked, grabbing the shelves where they stored their gear and dragging it against the door. North got hold of the other end and pushed.

"That's not going to be enough," North said.

Wha-whump!

The next assault made the hinges of the door cry out in distress.

Nichols and C-Rod made it to the entrance. They were breathless and confused.

"I thought Sherm said the earthquake was over," C-Rod gasped.

North pointed at the door. "That's no earthquake. It's them."

Wha-whump!

Again, everything rattled.

"That door's not gonna hold much longer," Dallas said.

"We need to fill the room," Nichols said. The entrance to the base was comprised of a small prep room.

"With what?" C-Rod said.

"Anything solid. Create an impenetrable wall."

North knew exactly what he meant. If they jammed the room full of stuff, even if the hinges broke, the door wouldn't be able to open.

"Let's go," North said to Dallas. They hustled to the supply room just across the way, grabbing more heavy shelving. Under normal circumstances, North would have a hard time moving them, complaining about his bad back all the way, but adrenaline was making easy work of it. Nichols and C-Rod lugged a steel file cabinet and chairs. The four men went back and forth, dragging the heaviest, sturdiest furniture they could find, the haphazard pile growing fast.

All the while the pounding on the door and the wall around the door continued. North desperately wanted to look through the window to see if any of the men had been wounded or even better, killed, in their lust to get inside. Getting to the window in the door was impossible now, thanks to the tangle of debris filling the room.

Sweating profusely (*I don't think I've broken a sweat since I got here*, North thought), North wedged the last item that would fit into the room: Holli's dresser. The entrance/prep room was filled wall to wall and floor to ceiling – a solid block of scrap.

Dallas leaned against the wall, his gun pointed into the room. "Think that'll keep them out?"

North arched an eyebrow. "We better hope it does." His heart slammed so hard, he could hear its wild beating in his ringing ears.

Wha-whump.

"Sounds like they're running out of steam," Nichols said.

He was right. That one barely shook this part of the base.

"Jeannie, what does it look like out there?" Nichols said into his walkie.

"They just took out the camera mounted by the entrance," she replied, her voice high and worried. "Before they did, we watched them drag some of their men away, past the light. They looked hurt."

"I don't doubt it," North said. "They attacked like battering rams." He imagined broken bones, internal bleeding, massive head wounds. All of them richly deserved.

"Can you spot them on any other cameras?" Nichols asked.

There was a pause. "No."

"Have Holli and Sherm check the windows. We're coming back."

"What about the door?" Jeannie asked.

Dallas put his walkie close to his mouth. "Darling, they're not getting in that door without dynamite."

Everyone remained glued to the monitors, with C-Rod doing rounds, checking windows. The remaining bat men, and there were plenty, had ceased their assault. Dallas kept watch on them by the window with nothing much to report. They had ceased all movement, heads bowed, shoulders slumped.

"Like toys that had their batteries removed," Dallas said.

Through it all, the winds picked up, the distant rumble of the storm not so distant anymore. Jeannie had stopped checking on it because what was the point? They had a far greater concern out there, seemingly waiting for them.

"I don't even care what they are at this point," Holli said. "I just want to know where the hell they came from."

"It's snowing men?" Sherm said. Even he looked disgusted with himself for trying to make light of their situation.

"I'm not giving a hallelujah on that one," C-Rod said as he entered the room. "You ask me, they're from space. I bet there's some crashed ship out there under the ice where they've been hiding out."

Nichols was dead tired. The rushes of adrenaline had left him in total crash mode. He swiveled his chair and narrowed his eyes at C-Rod. "That's the movie, *The Thing*. You better hope it's not like that."

"Never heard of it." C-Rod poured himself a coffee and opened a pack of Twinkies.

Nichols didn't have the strength to explain. The ground snow was swirling, making it hard to see anything. Those men could be everywhere, but the building winds were giving them perfect cover.

They were all clinging to the hope that the storm would be too much for the bat men to endure. If there was anyone listening to their prayers, they would be gone, carried away by the freakish winds.

Something told Nichols that wasn't going to happen. Dallas confided to him that he felt the same way. Those things were perfectly suited to Antarctica. The cold and dark and high winds were, to them, the same as a day on the beach to the humans inside Freedom Base.

But what did they want?

Obviously it wasn't shelter. Was it food? They looked well fed and healthy, despite their pallid flesh. Unless they didn't crave food in the traditional sense. The succeeding thought made Nichols visibly shiver.

"Sherm, Holli, C-Rod, why don't you all try to get some shut eye," he said. "We'll take turns keeping watch."

"Like hell I will," Jeannie said. "You look like the one that needs a week of sleep. I couldn't close my eyes now if you drugged me."

He looked at his wife and her squared posture and knew there was no bucking this bull. Nichols raised his hands, palms out. "Okay, me, Holli and C-Rod will hit the hay." The other two didn't protest. "We'll set our alarms for three hours from now. Sound good?"

Jeannie squeezed his arm. "The only thing that would sound good right now is a rescue plane."

"Or a tank," C-Rod said.

Nichols' back cracked as he rose from the chair. He glanced at North, who looked pretty beat. "You want to knock off now? You look like you could use it."

North waved him off. "I'll be fine. Not doing much other than sitting anyway. I'd offer you each a sleeping pill, but it wouldn't wear off in three hours."

"Suit yourself."

The walk to their rooms seemed longer than ever. The wind kicked into high gear, wailing at the walls of the base. C-Rod trudged to his quarters without speaking a word, which was very unusual for him. Holli lingered beside Nichols.

"Where do you think they're from?" she asked, barely above a whisper.

"Not from Mars," he replied. "Other than that, one guess is as good as another."

"You think they'll get in?"

He was tempted to blow smoke up her ass, but the way her eyes were piercing his own, as if she were scouring his soul, he knew it was better to shoot straight. "If they want to, they will. They don't seem to even care how much it would hurt them or worse. We just have to be grateful they don't have any weapons or tools."

Holli broke away, staring down the empty corridor. "Weapons," she said before shuffling off to her room.

Nichols closed his door behind him and collapsed on the bed. His brain was on fire but his body was done. He fell asleep in seconds.

The rattling of the storm woke C-Rod up. He checked his watch. He'd only been asleep for an hour.

"Son of a bitching storm," he muttered, turning over.

The cacophony was impossible to ignore. Each rumble of wind made him think those naked assholes were launching another assault.

He needed sleep. They all did. If they had to fight to stand their ground, they would be at a major disadvantage if they were delirious and weak from exhaustion.

C-Rod reached under his bed for his laptop and powered it up. He went to a folder labeled CLASSICS and opened it, revealing file after file of old school porn. He preferred the classics from the 80s and early 90s. The porn stars today always shaved themselves to within an inch of their lives. He preferred his porn to be a little more natural. He found one with Christy Canyon and Jennifer Stewart, two of his favorites, and pulled his pants down.

At times when he was wound up and couldn't sleep, C-Rod found a quick jerk session was all he needed to drift off to slumber land. Truth be told, he jerked off when he was tired, happy, sad and angry. It was better than drugs and he wasn't hurting anyone, except himself on days when he was short on lube.

Christy and Jennifer were about to get on opposite ends of a dildo the size of a pogo stick when something struck the base so hard, one of his shelves came crashing off the wall.

C-Rod jumped too, his laptop hitting the floor with a loud crack, Christy and Jennifer's moans instantly silenced. Tucking himself in, C-Rod stood in the middle of his room, waiting.

The wind was loud and constant. Someone could have been calling to him through the door and he might not have heard them.

His muscles tight, insides coiled like a snake in a charmer's basket, he waited for the other shoe to drop.

It didn't take long.

CHAPTER TWELVE

Dallas had lost sight of the men through the driving snow. It wasn't until they were less than ten feet from the base that they became visible, silent wraiths emerging from the white out. They leapt and hurled their bodies at the outer wall. As the first line of men fell, the next line took their place, hammering the structure like lemmings.

"Oh no."

His first instinct was to smash the window and start shooting. They were so close and tightly packed, it would be impossible to miss. He squeezed the handle of the gun, tempted, but common sense won out. He didn't have anywhere near enough bullets to take them all out, and if he shattered that window, they were all fucked in a very different way.

"It's them!" he shouted down the hall.

Jeannie, North and Sherm came running to him.

"I was hoping it was the storm," Sherm said.

They gathered by the window, jumping back when the next barrage hit, shaking the wall.

"Hope is starting to become a four letter word around here," Dallas said.

"They may have been waiting for the storm to make their attack," North said. "The combined forces should be enough to cause a breach."

Dallas looked at Jeannie, the both of them flushed with dread.

Sherm looked outside again. "How are they even able to stand upright? The wind should be tossing them around like dolls."

"They may be heavier than they look," Dallas said. "From what I can see, they're solid muscle." So solid, he wondered if a bullet from the Glock would even do much damage. If he did have to shoot, it would have to be headshots, preferably getting them in their oversized eyes. That wouldn't be easy to do with moving targets. "Like zombies," he muttered.

Thankfully, no one heard him.

The bat men rammed the outer walls over and over. Even though this part of the base was elevated, they were still going to eventually crush the part they could reach.

"What's happening now?" Nichols said, his shirt unbuttoned and shoes in his hand.

Jeannie ran to him. "They're at it again and they won't stop."

Nichols looked out the window, steadying himself when they slammed into the wall.

"Between them and the wind, this place is going to break apart," Dallas said.

C-Rod came in, followed by Holli who held an armload of sharp, pointed sticks.

"I couldn't sleep," she said. "So I made these." She had gathered every mop, broom and shovel she could find, whittling them down to make sturdy spears.

As the base vibrated, all eyes were on Nichols.

"Everybody, suit up," he said. "We have to be ready if they get through. It'll get deathly cold in here in seconds."

"And then what?" Sherm asked. "We can't ride out the winter wrapped in layers."

Unlike those things, Dallas thought.

"We'll burn that bridge when we get to it. Now hurry up!" Nichols grumbled.

Everyone left to get their gear but Dallas and Jeannie.

"You want me to stay here until you're all suited up?" Dallas asked.

"No. Go get dressed. They're going to keep at it whether you're watching them or not."

"I'm scared, Rob," Jeannie said.

He hugged her. "I know, honey. We all are. I'll find a way out of this." Nichols didn't sound so sure of himself because he wasn't.

Jeannie mercifully didn't ask him to make it a promise. The couple left the room hand in hand.

Dallas took one last look out the window. He saw open wounds on the heads of some of the bat men. They hit so hard, a tiny spider web of a crack etched itself in the glass.

It was a race now to see what would get in first – the bizarre men, or the brutal storm.

Holli had given a spear to Sherm, North and C-Rod before they headed to their rooms to layer up. She was thankful she had gone to the entrance room to get her clothes out of the dresser that had been stuffed in there earlier. With everything on the floor, it was easy to see what she needed.

She shimmied out of her jeans and slipped into thick long johns.

Whittling the spears had calmed her. When she'd first started working on the shovel, she could barely hold her knife. But the more she shaved away at the wood, the more her hands steadied themselves. And with that came a wave of, if not placidity, at least quiet.

"I am not going to die down here," she said, pulling two shirts and a sweater over her head.

She opened her night table drawer and took out her flashlight along with two spare batteries. Light was going to be as essential as a weapon if they had to go outside.

"I am not going to die down here."

Her Big Red coat was draped over a chair, a balaclava on the seat.

Holli remembered the day she'd finally stood up to her stepfather, telling him that if he hit her again, she was going to first hurt him, then report him to the police. The son of a bitch had laughed, his cigarette and coffee teeth belittling her bravado. He'd patted his belt and took a step towards her, only too happy to show her the error of her logic. At least until she'd brandished the carving knife she'd hidden behind her back.

"I hear there's a major artery by your balls. How about I make you a eunuch? You won't have to mourn the small, very small, loss for long though. You'll bleed out before you get to really cry about it. Not that it would be much of a loss."

"You wouldn't dare."

Holli strode across the room and pushed the tip of the blade into his crotch, the denim a thin wall between life and death. "I wouldn't have, at least until you came into my life."

She couldn't believe the words coming out of her mouth, nor the strength and self-assuredness behind them. The sudden flash of fear in his cold, dead eyes only encouraged her more. She pushed the knife a little further. As he stepped back, he tripped over the edge of her bed and fell, his head thumping against the floor.

"Now get the hell out of my room!" she shouted. "And don't ever think of coming near me again. In fact, get the fuck out of my house. If you so much as touch my mother, I'll kill you."

She'd expected some sort of protest, but he simply got up and left. A half an hour later, Holli watched him load his bags in his piece of shit Corolla and tear ass down the street, never to return.

Her mother had been devastated at his leaving them, even knowing that he'd been taking his hands to Holli on a weekly basis. It was then that Holli had decided her mother was just as toxic as that abusive slime ball. After she graduated high school, she left and never went back. The following years had been filled with adventure, fear, revelations and moments of loss and terror. But she persevered.

Despite everything happening now with death breathing down the back of her neck, she still wouldn't wish to be back home with her mother.

She would survive this. It's what she did best.

CHAPTER THIRTEEN

Rob and Jeannie Nichols suited up in record time, helping one another into extra layers, but not so many that it would restrict their ability to move. He had a strong feeling they'd need full mobility of their arms and legs.

Jeannie was putting on her wool hat when she said, "Remember how you wanted kids and I said we would when I was good and ready?"

Nichols winced. That had been a sore spot with them over the past few years. Rob had had a harrowing tour in Afghanistan and was content with settling down in the suburbs with a minivan full of children. Hell, he'd be happy as a clam to see Jeannie wearing elastic waistband mommy jeans, the two of them too tired to stay awake past nine o'clock.

Jeannie had other plans. Her thirst for adventure hadn't been quenched. He was beginning to wonder if it ever would. Visions of holding his daughter's tiny hand on walks around the neighborhood had been growing fuzzy and remorseful for the loss of something he'd never have.

"Yeah," he said, looking for his insulated gloves.

She cupped his face in her gloved hands. "When we get out of this, you can make as many Irish twins as you want." Her eyes shimmered with tears.

He pulled down their balaclavas and kissed her. "Then we better not let Liam and Faith down."

Jeannie looked at him quizzically. He kissed her again. When he pulled away, he saw that she understood.

"Can I at least name our son? I'm not crazy about Liam."

"Anything but Rob Junior."

The entire base rattled as the high winds and frantic bat men hammered its walls. Jeannie picked up the spear Holli had made for her. "Let's go. Dean's not going to get made with us standing here." She strode out of the room, Nichols close behind her.

One thing he'd learned in the service – you needed something beyond yourself to live for.

God help those bat men for wanting to come between Rob and Jeannie and their future children.

North had been the first to return to the storage room. He was grateful not to feel a whistling, icy wind emanating from the doorway. Though it was disheartening to see the cracked window. That wouldn't last long at all. They could shut the door, but those men would just get inside and smash it to pieces.

"Holding steady?" Sherm asked breathlessly. His trademark dreads were tucked away, only his wide eyes and bridge of his nose visible. North had yet to put his headgear on. He didn't want to get all sweaty inside and then have it freeze if they had to abandon the camp.

"So far," North said. "You should remove all that." He pointed at Sherm's hood, hat and balaclava. "You get all kinds of condensation in there now, it'll be solid ice in seconds."

"Shit. Right." Sherm quickly ripped it all off, his dreads spilling across his shoulders. He had a spear in each hand. North almost chuckled, the vision of this Rasta, peaceable, geek scientist looking like a warrior.

"You ready to do some spear fishing?" North asked.

"No. But I'll do what I have to."

The others arrived seconds later. Everyone was armed with a spear but Dallas, who had the gun. North wondered why Nichols hadn't taken the gun by now, considering he was in charge and was the designated bearer of arms. Though Dallas *had* served in the Marines, so both men knew exactly what they were doing when it came to firearms. The last time North had fired a weapon was at a rifle range on his honeymoon too many years ago to count. He hadn't been a good shot then and he would be ten times worse now.

Glancing into the room, he saw that the wall had dented, irregular lumps everywhere he looked. Pretty soon, the metal would give way and then it was game over.

As if reading his mind, Nichols said, "They can't all get in at once. In fact, they're going to have to work at it just to get a single breach to widen. C-Rod and I will position ourselves on either side of the breach. We'll spear any that try to come in. Maybe we can clog up the works with their bodies. Any other breaks start to happen, we'll need two people around them to do the same. I know it doesn't feel like it at the moment, but we have the advantage here."

The thundering at the wall dashed any hopes that North could believe him. Not that he was particularly afraid of dying. Truth be told, he was good and ready. There wasn't a day that went by when he didn't miss his Linda. He'd seen enough people die, especially during his residency, that he knew in his heart there was more to life than hunkering inside a meat sack for seventy or so years. He was intrigued to find out what came next, and confident he would find Linda.

That didn't mean he would go down without a fight. He was a doctor because he wanted to save lives, and there were six other lives that needed him now to make sure they played out their string on this big blue marble. There would be trepidation and guilt over killing another human being, but he wasn't so sure those things outside were or ever had been human.

Wham!

The sound of tearing steel chilled his blood.

A pale, thick-veined hand punched through the rent in the wall.

Before Nichols or C-Rod could react, North hustled into the room and ran his spear through the hand. The fingers shot straight out. He could feel them quiver through the spear's handle. He pulled the spear free, flecks of blood painting the wall. The hand disappeared.

He wished he could hear the thing on the other side howling with pain, but the only sound possible in the confined space now was the high whistling of the wind as it rushed icy death into the base.

C-Rod gaped at the blood spatter on the wall. He had to shout above the screeching wind. "At least we know they bleed red like us. I was beginning to wonder if they had weird green shit running through their veins."

The smell of copper and ice assaulted North's nose. He donned his balaclava, both as protection against the cold and to filter the strong scent.

"Here comes another!" C-Rod exclaimed.

This time, what came through was a fist, punching hard enough to allow the bat-man to get his arm up to his elbow inside. Nichols stomped on the elbow joint, the wicked crack piercing through the wind. C-Rod stabbed its arm and hand several times. The arm went slack, rivers of blood running onto the floor. Then suddenly it was gone, as if one of the other men had tugged the man away.

They waited, but nothing tried to come in.

The temperature in the room plummeted.

The pounding had ceased.

Dallas was on one knee in a shooter's stance, the gun aimed at the gap in the wall.

"Whatever comes through, don't shoot," Nichols said. "Save the bullets for when we really need them."

"You be sure to tell me when that is," Dallas replied.

North knew how he felt. If this wasn't the time, he shuddered to think when it would be.

Holli and Jeannie dragged a heavy box and jammed it against the hole, muting the ear-piercing wind. "If the box moves, slide it over and start making them see the error of their ways," Holli said.

"I think they already did," North said. His breath curled out of his mouth, hanging above Sherm's head for a moment before dissipating.

The light outside the lone window blinked out.

"Shit," Nichols spat. He went to the window, shining his flashlight through the damaged glass. "I don't see them."

C-Rod took up a small section of the window, his head moving back and forth. "Me neither. Where the hell did they go?"

"The cameras," North said. He sprinted to the control room, Jeannie right behind him. His chest felt tight, his legs not his own. Fear of what he and Jeannie would see on the monitors nipped at his heels, tickling the back of his neck. He nearly tore the door off its hinges.

Jeannie groaned.

North's eyes danced across the monitors while his heart skittered and thumped painfully.

Staggered from what he saw, he slumped against a table.

"God help us."

CHAPTER FOURTEEN

"Rob, get in here!"

Nichols grabbed his walkie and looked to Dallas. "Take my spot. Everyone else, sit tight."

He gave Dallas his spear and ran.

The second he stepped into the control room, he knew something was wrong – or more wrong in this case. North looked as if he'd just been punched in the gut, intentionally looking away from the monitors. Jeannie stood with her hands on her hips, her face contorted in either pain or deep concentration.

He was about to ask what had happened when his eyes slid to what was being played out on the monitors.

"Please tell me you're playing some sci-fi movie," he said.

Jeannie shook her head. "What are those things?"

North spoke up, his voice raspy, "Nothing anyone's ever seen before. If someone did, they didn't live to tell the tale, that's for shit sure."

Nichols' throat went dry as a desert. It hurt to swallow.

Three of the monitors were filled from end to end with the impossible. He couldn't wrap his brain around what he was seeing, much less form any coherent words. All he was able to manage was, "We're – "

"Fucked," North finished for him. "We're good and fucked, Nichols."

"We're not going to be able to keep them out," Jeannie said with calm certainty.

She was right. What had surrounded them would not be stopped by mere walls, triple reinforced windows and doors. Not against that. No, certainly not.

"Everyone has to see this," Nichols said. He noticed that the cameras and lights were rocking in the high winds. How long until they snapped off and they were essentially blind? A couple had already bitten the dust, a wall of pitch black filing the monitors. It was better that they all knew what they were up against.

"But what about the storage room?" Jeannie asked.

"That's the least of our worries." He keyed his walkie. "Dallas, bring everyone to the control room."

His reply crackled, "Everyone? Who's gonna watch out for those bastards trying to come in?"

Nichols wavered. Maybe he should leave two people in storage, just in case those men made another attempt to get in. But what he was seeing outside told him the gathering of bat men had decided to try another approach, one that wouldn't be thwarted by homemade spears and a lone gun.

"Forget it. I need you all here."

There was a long pause, then, "Copy."

It was a lone word, but Nichols heard the resignation in Dallas' voice. The grizzled vet knew when things went from bad to worse.

"What do you think they want with us?" Jeannie said. She'd taken a seat in front of the monitors, panning the cameras to see as much as they could in the artificial light.

"They want us out there, with them. I don't think they understand that we're not built to survive these temperatures. For all I know, they think everyone and everything that can traipse around in an Antarctic winter is normal. The question is, do we go out there, or make them come in and get us?"

North straightened up. "You can't be serious! You expect us to walk out there and say hello?"

Nichols massaged the back of his neck. He needed painkillers. The tension in his neck and back was radiating talons of pain that raked across his brain. "If we do that, maybe we can save the base, have something to come back to on the off chance they just wanted to see our smiling faces and walk away. If we don't, we freeze to death even if they don't mean us harm."

The doctor strode across the small room and pounded the wall. "I hate it when you're right."

Nichols nodded at Jeannie. "Not as much as she does."

Her silence told volumes. If she thought she could poke a hole in his theory, she would have done so by now.

"The question is, who will make up the welcoming committee?"

"As a man with some Native American in my blood, the last time we met white men, things did not go well for the non-white men," North said.

Jeannie pointed at the monitor, at the clustered gathering of the uber pale bat men. "Well, they certainly beat us in the white department."

Dallas, Holli, C-Rod and Sherm filed into the control room, any protests about leaving their important post dying on their lips the moment they saw the foreboding tableau on the monitors.

C-Rod rubbed his eyes until the rims were red. "Am I fucking seeing this right?"

Holli's hand went straight to her open mouth. "I…what are those?"

Sherm dropped into the chair beside Jeannie. He began using the controls on camera two to zoom in on the focus of Holli's attention.

When it turned to face the camera, Dallas stuffed the gun in his pocket. "Might as well be a pea shooter."

The creature seemed to glare at them with pale eyes as blue as ice. Two of the bat men sat on the beast's wooly back. There were no reins or saddle. Nichols wondered how the men managed to stay atop it, much less control it.

"It looks like a bunch of things," Holli said. "That snout, that's a polar bear. But the body's too big. It looks like paintings I've seen of baby wooly mammoths. Those ears, the tail, even the paws, I'm thinking snow leopard. It's all of those but none of them."

There had to be dozens of those creatures outside their door. Most had riders, but others stood stock-still, thick plumes of frozen air expelling from their nostrils and open mouths. They didn't look friendly.

"I thought those guys were freaky, but their pets take the cake," C-Rod said.

He wasn't far off calling them pets. If they were wild beasts, Nichols would expect them to either run from or attack the throng of identical men. They were more like horses – terrifying chimeras of impossibility thriving in an equally impossible environment.

"What are they waiting for?" Sherm said, his eyes big as ping pong balls.

"Nichols thinks they're waiting for us," North said.

"Us?" Dallas said. "What do you mean, us?"

"I'm going out there to see what they want," Nichols said. It was the last thing on Earth he wanted to do, but he'd set his mind that it was the right thing to do.

"I highly doubt they speak English," C-Rod said. "How the hell will you even be able to communicate with them?"

Holli stepped between Nichols and Dallas. "By showing them you're not afraid. And that you're also not a threat. I'd like to come with you."

Nichols had always suspected that Holli was tougher than a five-dollar steak, but the resolve in her eyes told him he'd underestimated her.

"She's right," Jeannie said. "But I'm not sure Holli should go with you. There are no women out there. We don't know how they'll react to her, or me if I go."

Dallas huffed and waved his hand. "They won't even be able to tell what you are under all that gear."

"Maybe we all should go," C-Rod said. The maintenance tech was a hothead, but Nichols wondered if he was all talk. He couldn't take the chance of the man showing off the size of his balls if things got tense out there.

"No," Nichols said. "I don't want them knowing how few of us are stationed here. Let them think the base is full of people. Sherm, I'd like you to come."

"Me? Why me?"

"Because you're smart. You might be able to see and understand things better than me."

The scientist got up, his dreads fanning as he spun around. "Oh, I see. The black guy is expendable. Just toss him out there so mega-whitey can feed him to those things."

Nichols leaned against the wall, his eyes flicking to the monitors. "Quit being dramatic and don't even think of playing the race card with me. I told you why and that's the truth of it. And I'm not asking. So let's go."

CHAPTER FIFTEEN

It took some effort to remove all of the stuff they'd piled into the entrance room. Everyone lent a hand but Jeannie, whom Nichols asked to stay in the control room and keep an eye on things. The entire time he was removing furniture and boxes, he felt the passing of each second. How many grains of sand were left in the glass before the small army of oddness out there took action?

When they were done, Nichols told Holli and Sherm to go back to their rooms and change. They'd sweat through their clothes and needed to be dry as a hangover mouth to go outside.

Nichols tied himself to Holli and Sherm. He wasn't even sure they'd be able to stand upright for more than five seconds. The wind was getting worse. His concern that the guideline would snap, sending them off into the freezing darkness to die, couldn't be overstated.

But they had to go out there.

"Here, let me adjust your goggles," he said to Holli. He pulled the black elastic straps tighter.

"Are you trying to weld it to my face?" she complained.

"Actually, yes. You don't want anything getting in there."

The snow was driving so hard, it could easily blind them.

Sherm picked up his spear.

"Leave it," Nichols said.

"Are you crazy?"

"They don't have weapons and we're not going to have weapons."

"This is no time to go all peace and love. You see those animals they brought? If they aren't weapons, I don't know what is."

Dallas bustled into the room. "I think what he means is not to have any visible weapons." He handed the Glock to Nichols. "Just in case."

Nichols nodded, stuffing the gun in the pocket of his Big Red. Dallas clapped him on the shoulder and left.

"Put your lights on," Nichols said.

They clicked their headlamps on as well as the high-powered flashlights they each held.

Nichols had his hand on the doorknob, but before he turned it, he said to Sherm, “You think that oversized toothpick is going to stop one of those from stomping or eating you?”

Sherm thought it over and his shoulders slumped.

“If it makes you feel any better,” Nichols said, ”I have the gun.”

What he didn’t add was that his gloves were so thick, he’d never be able to get his finger inside the trigger guard. He’d have to remove his glove to shoot, and the moment he did, his hand would have seconds before it froze solid.

“You all ready?”

Holli nodded.

Sherm said, “Not now, not ever.”

“Okay then.”

He opened the door and they were instantly slammed in the face by the wind. The cold knifed through their layers, chilling them.

Nichols attached them to the guideline. They’d have to turn the right corner to get to the nearest of the bat men and their beasts. It was only a few feet, but it would feel like a mile. A powerful gust of wind almost took his legs out from under him. Holli slammed into his back, Sherm into hers.

“We look like the Three Stooges,” he said, but his words were ripped from his lips and scattered into the ether. It would be impossible to hear one another out here.

Nichols paused to make sure he had his footing, and then proceeded slowly.

As he inched around the edge of the massive pillars that supported this end of the building, his light fell on a smooth, alabaster face. The man didn’t even blink his solid black eyes or raise a hand to shield them. In fact, he didn’t move at all. Nichols was inclined to poke the man with his flashlight to see if perhaps they had lucked out and he had turned into an ice sculpture. Then he saw the man’s chest move with a shallow intake of breath and he was grateful he’d held back.

The wind didn’t care about what was happening out here. It bullied Nichols, Holli and Sherm. They teetered and tottered, looking like weak babies learning to walk. With verbal communication impossible, they were not presenting themselves in the best light.

Show them you’re not afraid, Holli had said. *And you’re not a threat.*

They had the latter down in spades. As for not looking afraid, the only thing the bat men would be able to see was their eyes, and the goggles would make that hard to do.

We must look as alien to them as they do to us.

He worried about making any wild gestures that could be misinterpreted. With the wind trying to constantly knock them down, it was hard not to flail their arms.

Hugging the supports, they fought for a few more feet, coming face to face with the phalanx of men and monsters. The creatures were the most terrifying things Nichols had ever seen. Now that they were up close, he could see their mouths were crammed with huge, sharp teeth. Their oversized eyes were so crystal, they pierced the endless night like headlights.

Just what in the holy hell were they?

Nichols stopped, his legs straining, knees locked. He stared back at them, Holli and Sherm doing the same. None of the bat men came forward. Nor did they attack, which was a good thing.

There were other packs like this at other points around the base. Nichols wondered if he'd chosen the wrong one. Perhaps the man in authority, if such a thing existed, was elsewhere.

Holli raised a hand in greeting.

The bat men reacted by tilting their heads in unison, intrigued by her hand's movement.

Nichols didn't know what was more unsettling – the ferocious looking creatures or the hive behavior of the men.

He took Holli's cue and did the same. The heads tilted the other way.

One of the animals pawed the snowy ground, mimicking a bull before it charged. Nichols felt his stomach fold in on itself. If it rushed them, they would be stomped to bits.

A screaming gale shoved Nichols sideways. He, Holli and Sherm toppled to the ground.

The bat men's heads snapped upright. Their eyes grew even wider. The animals snorted.

Holli grabbed Nichols' hood as he struggled to get up. The simple gesture urged him to do so slowly. He took a deep breath, the cold stabbing his lungs, coughed, and got on all fours. With some effort, he rose to his feet.

One of the bat men strode toward them. Nichols saw he had no nipples or navel. He was as smooth as a doll, with the exception of his pendulous, swaying member.

Nichols braced himself. He wanted to reach into his pocket for the irrational comfort of the gun but didn't want to make any suspicious moves.

He also desperately wanted to be able to talk to Holli and Sherm, but it was impossible.

The man stopped just a foot away from Holli. To her credit, she didn't back up. He raised his hand, his index finger pointing at her, and tapped her goggles. Nichols almost lunged at him, but a sharp breeze practically sent him sprawling in the other direction.

Holli flinched, but stood her ground.

He then moved to Sherm and did the same. Sherm made to swat his hand away and the bat-man shot a glance at his rising arm, as if to say, 'I will break your arm if you touch me.'

Sherm checked himself.

Rob waited for the man to do the same to him, but he turned his back on them instead.

Now what?

Rob considered approaching the bat-man when their collective mouths opened. Swirling mist flowed from their open maws as they tilted their heads back as far as they could go. The eerie, high-pitched screech they made overwhelmed the storm's fury. All Rob wanted to do was run like hell and get back inside the base. The tug on his line showed that was exactly what Sherm was doing.

The howling of the men was joined by the strange beasts.

Rob's heart pounded as the Antarctic night was ripped in two by the wailing creatures that surely were not men.

CHAPTER SIXTEEN

Jeannie Nichols could hear the army of men and creatures through the base's walls.

"That doesn't sound good," C-Rod said from his perch behind her.

She scanned the monitors and saw that the mysterious interlopers from all sides of Freedom Base had joined in the chorus.

"No, no it doesn't," she said. "Come on, Rob, get out of there."

Why wasn't he moving? It looked like Sherm had attempted to get back inside, but Holli and Rob were holding firm.

"I can go out there and get them," Dallas said. He was already tugging on his wool hat and slipping a headlamp over it.

"Wait," Jeannie said. "Not yet."

Rob had told her that he would give her a sign if they needed any help. That sign would be him tapping the top of his head. His arms were by his side, flailing out every now and then to fight the wind. She wished to hell he had let her go out with him. As terrifying as it would be, she'd rather be next to him than watching helplessly through a camera feed.

"What are we waiting for?" Dallas insisted.

Jeannie said, "Please. Just wait." She couldn't hide the tension and irritation in her voice.

Her heart flipped when the men and their chimeric animals stopped at the same time.

"Jesus, how do they do that?" C-Rod said.

"It's like they have one mind," North said. He'd been drinking from a flask he'd gotten from his room. Jeannie wasn't sure what was in it, but judging by his breath, it was high octane. She knew there was no point telling the doctor how ill advised it was to hit the bottle now. As a matter of fact, she was finding it increasingly difficult to not ask for a hit. "I can see members of the same species having some sort of link, but not two disparate species. Maybe we're just not quick enough to see those things taking their cue from the men. But to my eyes, it looks like they're acting as one at the exact same moment."

Jeannie zoomed in on Rob, Holli and Sherm. Their backs were to the camera, their bodies wavering back and forth as the wind pushed them around. "I want to know what that all meant."

"I don't think that was the Antarctic version of Kumbaya," Dallas said. "I'm getting them." He angrily jammed his arms into his Big Red coat.

The floor began to vibrate.

Jeannie looked to the monitors. The bat men weren't moving.

"Aftershock," she said.

"Come on, C-Rod," Dallas shouted, running out of the control room.

"Right behind you."

The shaking grew worse.

Jeannie watched in helpless horror as Rob fell backwards, pulling Holli and Sherm with him. "Please don't touch them," she whispered. She jumped when North clamped a hand over her shoulder.

"Look," he said.

The bat men and the creatures were dispersing, walking backwards and out of the light.

The aftershock kept intensifying.

"Maybe the earthquake is scaring them off," North said.

Jeannie thought she was going to be sick. "I don't think they're scared of anything."

She had nothing to base it on other than the fact that they were the most frightening things she'd ever beheld. What on Earth could scare something that belonged in your worst nightmares?

Instead of leveling off, the aftershock, like the storm, grew worse and worse. Jeannie heard things falling off the shelves but couldn't tear herself away from the monitors to look. Then the image on the monitors started to grow fuzzy and blink.

"Crap, the tremors must be loosening the connections." She unleashed a string of expletives that would have made her husband blush.

Now the rack where the monitors were mounted was swaying. Something popped and fizzled behind them. She smelled the acrid stench of burning wires.

"We need to get under a doorway," North said, trying to pull her from her seat.

Jeannie watched her husband as he tried to get up. Each time he got close, the shifting earth sent him back down.

And then the monitors blinked out. Crashing and clattering echoed throughout the base. The lights dimmed, came back on.

And then went out.

All Sherm wanted to do was get off his ass and double time it back into the illusionary safety of the base. The waves of aftershocks weren't helping one damn bit. At least it had frightened off the un-welcoming committee.

"Come on, Holli," he shouted, but there was no way she could hear him. His balaclava was starting to freeze over. Once it did, it would be increasingly harder to breathe.

The ground kept rumbling and he was beginning to think this was no aftershock, but another earthquake. If he could get inside and to his equipment, he'd know. He tugged on the line that connected him to Holli. She was on her side, rolling in the snow.

An enormous thump directly under them sent Sherm onto his side as well.

What the hell?

He'd never experienced anything like that during a quake. It was like having an angry old man underneath them banging on the ceiling with a broom. A very, very big broom.

Sherm looked around them, resigned to the fact that this is where he was going to be riding out the tremors. The pale men and their ugly pets were gone. Of course, they could just be twenty feet away, cloaked in darkness, watching.

Glancing up, he watched the light pole sway, the cone of light roving over the icy, snowy ground like the spotlight at the circus.

When it started to flicker, Sherm somehow managed to jump to his feet, a jolt of adrenaline making his heart gallop like a thoroughbred. He grabbed Holli's Big Red and yanked her to her feet, pulling her close so she didn't fall again. He spread his legs apart, riding the shifting ground like a surfer.

"Take my hand!" he screamed at Nichols, who may not have heard him, but understood. Sherm had no time for wonder and pride when they were all back on their pins. This time, *he* led the way, pulling on the guideline, fighting the biting wind and time, inching toward the door.

When the lights blinked out, he cried out, grateful Holli and Nichols couldn't hear his less than manly reaction. Their headlamps and flashlights seemed utterly insignificant.

Why couldn't I have studied earthquakes in Indonesia or Mexico? The worst I'd get there is a sunburn and a few hangovers from cocktail hour.

The allure of the South Pole had been too great a pull for him. How many seismologists would get this chance? At the time, he couldn't say no. He'd always felt like a bit of a misfit, and this place was custom made for misfits or adrenaline junkies.

He could certainly say no now.

Holli shoved into his back and he turned to see Nichols pushing them all forward. Sherm got moving, leaning into the base's outer wall for support. He was afraid to swing his flashlight into the gloom lest he see those things had come back.

Just concentrate on getting back inside and figuring out how to get the power back on.

If the lights were out, so was the heat. The interior of the base would get as cold as the exterior before they knew it.

Sherm picked up his pace. He punched at his balaclava to break up the ice and allow more air, as much as it hurt, into his tired lungs.

When his light touched on the door just five feet away, Holli slapped his shoulder. He whooped with relief.

The earthquake must have sensed they were getting close, so it sent up a powerful wave of convulsions, nearly toppling them all over.

Sherm refused to go down. Not when they were this close. The wind joined in, making it impossible to take another step. It held them in frozen limbo.

His arm reached out as far as it would go, fingers desperate for the latch to open the door.

He spotted one of the flashlights angling to their right.

It just caught one of the great white beasts charging them. Sherm didn't have time to react.

The creature grazed his outstretched hand. Instead of hitting into them, it bashed the door to the base. The steel barrier folded in on itself, the frame cracking and widening. Half of the creature was in the base, its back legs still pumping to drive it in further.

There was nothing they could do to stop it.

They were, for all intents and purposes, dead.

CHAPTER SEVENTEEN

Dallas was glad he had his headlamp. He turned it on, the lone beam slashing through the sudden darkness. C-Rod was already hugging the doorframe. North had ahold of Jeannie, both of their eyes wide and round as frogs looking through thin ice.

First things first, they needed to be safe so they could ride out the quake.

"Come to me," he said, settling beside C-Rod. "Follow my light."

North and Jeannie smashed into the computer rack when a massive tremor nearly knocked the base on its side. Dallas gripped the doorframe to keep his footing. A chilling tendril of wind burned his face. The cold air must really be screaming through that rent in the wall in the storage room now. Or perhaps there was another break somewhere else. Dallas didn't even have time to worry about those men scrambling through the opening.

He put his hand out for North and Jeannie. She lashed out and grabbed his wrist. He pulled her to him. C-Rod managed to grab North. They huddled together in the tight space, listening to the base break apart.

"When is this gonna stop?" C-Rod exclaimed.

Only Sherm would be able to answer for sure, but Dallas was certain earthquakes didn't last too long. Hadn't he read that they typically only went on from ten to thirty seconds? This one was much longer than that, and it didn't feel as if it were losing steam.

What could only be described as an explosion rocked the base. Everyone stumbled out of the doorway, falling to their knees.

"What now?" C-Rod lamented.

It was followed by more concussions. The wind was now howling down the hall, freezing everything it touched.

"She's broken," Dallas said, referring to Freedom Base. "Get your gear on, now."

They grabbed their coats, hats and balaclavas, which wasn't easy in the dark. It took Dallas precious minutes to find their goggles that had fallen and slid under a table. They were going outside whether they liked it or not. If the entire base was compromised, he figured they wouldn't have long to panic…or suffer. They'd be dead soon enough.

He shined his light on spears that Holli had carved. They had fallen from the corner of the room and were splayed at their feet.

"Do we even bother?" North said.

"Hell yes, we bother," C-Rod said, grabbing one. He handed another to Jeannie who gratefully accepted the makeshift weapon. "If those things are outside, I'm taking as many down with me as I can."

Jeannie gave a solemn nod.

At least there were no illusions about survival with those two. Dallas was all for not going out quietly as well.

North plucked a spear from the floor. He didn't say a word and Dallas could barely see his face. But there was resignation in his body language.

"We have to go to Rob, Holli and Sherm," Jeannie said.

If they're still alive, Dallas thought.

They weren't faring so well inside the base. He couldn't imagine Nichols and his welcoming committee holding up under the unholy trinity of the earthquake, weather and the invaders.

"Now I know how Custer felt," he said, squaring up to face his fate. "You all stay behind me."

He expected to find a hallway filling with fine snow. His intention was to head for the entrance while assessing the damage. Did those men have dynamite? It sure as hell had sounded like it. If there was an off-chance Dallas could repair whatever had been damaged, he would stay behind and work at it while the rest went for Nichols, Holli and Sherm. Keeping the base alive meant hope for keeping themselves alive.

What he found instead was a corridor choked with the rushing bodies of the alabaster bat men. They came in a silent rush that scared Dallas more than anything else he'd seen in his entire life, combat missions where he was sure he was going to die included.

He tried to push his way back into the control room, but with the forward-moving bodies behind him, it was like coming up against a brick wall.

"Get back!" he screamed. "They're coming!"

Jeannie somehow slipped out from behind his back and froze at the sight of the rushing horde. The wind covered the sound of their heavy footfalls. Her mouth opened in a big, terrified O and was quickly filled with the hand of one of the bat men. He drove her to the ground, seemingly trying to choke her with his hand.

Dallas went to grab the back of the man's neck and was hit from behind. It felt like being tackled by a gorilla. As he fell, he twisted partway around, just in time to see a spear lash out in the space where his head had been a moment before. C-Rod impaled one of the men through the temple. As the dead man started to fall on Dallas, C-Rod went with him, refusing to relinquish his hold on the spear until he could tug it free from the man's shattered skull.

He heard North cry out a split-second before he was buried under a dog pile of the bat men. They flailed their fists and drove their hard-knobbed knees into every square inch of his body. Dallas tried to curl into a protective ball.

A particular shot to the bridge of his nose rang his bell. Everything went into soft focus and kept on dimming. Dallas fought to stay conscious, but in the end, passing out was a relief.

Nichols stared from the ground, aghast at the pile of alien men pouring into the base. He, Holli and Sherm were surrounded by the bizarre chimeras. He didn't need to speak their language to understand that if they moved, they were dead.

Deafened by the storm, he imagined the sounds of breaking glass, shattering wood and bending metal.

Worst of all, he kept hearing Jeannie's desperate cries running through his head, begging him to save her. He hoped to God she was alive and well enough to do just that, and damned that same God for separating them.

The shock kept him from worrying about hypothermia, which would be settling in soon enough. He did know he'd rather freeze to death than find himself in the jaws of the snorting creatures. Wishing for a merciful death seemed the only thing any of them could do right now. The South Pole was as unforgiving as a reptile. There was no room for error, and with Freedom Base being demolished just as the Amundsen-Scott Base had been obliterated, Nichols and his small crew were sure to meet the same fate.

At least you'll have fewer condolence letters and insurance payouts to send this time around, he thought bitterly of his bosses.

Holli reached for his hand and he took it. A gust of wind sent the trio sliding on their asses until their backs hit the warped base outer wall.

He did still have the gun.

Nichols knew it would be impossible to shoot their way out of this. Not that they had much in the way of firepower.

What he could do was save them from a grisly end. If needed, he would take out Holli, Sherm, and then look for Jeannie. But only when and if the time was right. He prayed he'd know it when it came. If there were no bullets left for him, then that would have to do. Most people didn't get to choose how they die, and no one was promised a peaceful, easy passing.

He took off his glove for a moment to feel around for the gun. The cold instantly went through his bones, turning his flesh to ice. Instead of putting his glove back on, he kept his hand thrust deep into his pocket, the Glock safely in his palm.

As if everything weren't bad enough, the ground rumbled mightily once again, the latest tremor lasting impossibly longer than the last. Nichols let go of the gun and grabbed Holli and Sherm by their jackets, holding them close as they bounced up and down as if they were in a child's jumping castle.

A piercing light blossomed on the horizon and for a moment, Nichols thought someone had dropped a nuclear bomb. The sudden burst of brilliance hurt his eyes and he had to quickly look away before it blinded him.

What the hell was going on in what was supposed to be one of the most uneventful sectors of the planet?

He squinted at Holli, saw her moving her mouth now that she'd pulled down her balaclava but couldn't read her lips through the light fog in his goggles.

The ground quaked, the base shook, the light faded, and the horrific creatures crept closer and closer.

CHAPTER EIGHTEEN

Once the pall of endless night returned, the unholy tremors ceased as well. Nichols raised his head and came face-to-face with one of the beasts. Its black lips were pulled back, fangs bared, dripping with saliva that froze at his feet. The glare from his headlamp bounced along the creature's nightmare-inducing visage.

Not daring to rise to his feet, he happily turned away to look at Freedom Base. The entire entryway had been reduced to rubble. Dozens of men stood before the wreckage, silent and waiting. But for what?

"The wind," Holli said.

At first, Nichols ignored her, thinking her voice was just another bit of conjuring in his head.

"It stopped," she added.

Now he did look at her. Her goggles sat high on her cap and her balaclava was yanked down under her chin, cracks and shards of ice hanging from it.

She was right. All of the madness had ceased in an instant. The sudden silence and stillness was more chilling than the weather.

"I think it's best we don't make any sudden moves," Nichols said, whispering. One of the beasts cocked its massive head as if trying to decipher his words.

"You don't have to tell me twice," Sherm said. The albino nose of one of the animals was sniffing at his Big Red. Sherm cowered against the wall, unable to get away from the inquisitive beast.

"Where are Jeannie and everyone else?" Holli asked. Her teeth were chattering.

It was the question that consumed Nichols. He didn't have an answer, so he didn't even try to provide one. He had a very strong, devastating suspicion, but he couldn't bring himself to voice it.

"You should shoot that one right between the eyes," Holli said, nodding at the creature closest to Nichols.

"What good would that accomplish?" he shot back, still keeping his voice down. The beast snorted, its vile breath invading his nose and lungs.

"Because I'll bet they've never seen or heard anything like it. Hit them with something unknown and they'll go running. Just like punching a bully in the face."

He looked at her as if she had become unhinged. Perhaps they all had. "These are no bullies, Hols. What's to say I shoot this one and the others go in for the kill?"

Holli looked to Sherm, his eyes wide and alert, then to the creatures and the men guarding the ruined entrance. "At least we go down fighting. Empty the gun in as many as you can and let's hope the religious nuts are right and we get a one way pass to Heaven for being murdered in a shit show like this."

He wanted to tell her she was crazy, but part of him suspected she might be right.

"I'm not doing a damn thing until I find out what happened to Jeannie."

"We may freeze to death before that happens," Sherm said. The light from his headlamp started to dim. How long would it be before they ran out of light as well?

A silent commotion rippled through the men. Their mouths opened and closed like gasping fish in eerie unison. The men closest to the entrance hustled backwards, shifting everyone else behind them.

One of them emerged, carrying a body over his shoulder. He dumped the body in the snow. Nichols was able to make out C-Rod's bloody and battered face. North was dropped beside him, followed by Dallas and Jeannie.

Dear God, Jeannie!

He couldn't tell if she was dead or alive.

Nichols jumped to his feet, prepared to run to her. The creature barreled its snout into his chest, sending him sprawling.

He pulled his hand from his pocket and shoved the gun in the animal's face. "Get the hell away from me," he shouted, as if it could understand him.

"Shoot it, Nichols!" Holli encouraged him. She had taken out a knife from her pocket and cut the rope connecting them. All sense of safety and common sense had flown the coop.

Nichols took a step toward where Jeannie and the others lay.

The creature stomped with him.

The men turned as one to stare at him.

"I mean it," he said, his breath curling like hookah smoke. He swiveled the gun at the men. They stared at it with their blank expressions and ebony eyes. His eyes flicked to Jeannie, looking for any sign she was still among the living.

Holli kept shouting at him to shoot. Sherm countered her commands by imploring him not to shoot.

His heart whapped against his ribcage. Despite the cold, sweat droplets formed and froze on his brow and upper lip.

What should he do?

It was wrong to endanger his entire crew just because he was concerned about his wife. It was the reason they rarely sent couples to the Pole. A conflict of interest could prove deadly down here.

Except they were already doomed.

And when he died, he wanted to do so beside Jeannie.

He took two long strides toward his wife's prone body.

Two of the creatures scampered to stand in his way, roaring so loud, it hurt his ears.

He roared back, not with his mouth, but with the barrel of his gun.

CHAPTER NINETEEN

The bullet tore through the eye of the beast closest to Nichols. Its eyeball popped with such force, it exploded like a geyser, painting Nichols with blood and viscera. The bizarre animal reared back onto its powerful hind legs and wailed, falling onto its back. It writhed on the ground with such ferocity, Nichols had to shove Holli and Sherm out of the way so they weren't crushed by its flailing limbs.

Holli had been right…partially. The other creatures backed away, but they hadn't fled. Nichols wasn't sure if they were frightened by the gun or the pained gyrations of their brethren. Even the bat men had trained their unsettling attention on the wounded beast, not one of them making a move to help it.

It didn't matter. It gave Nichols the opening to run to Jeannie.

Nichols slipped in his haste but was quick to regain his feet. He ripped his balaclava down, the cold biting his lips, making his teeth feel as if he'd bitten into a gallon of ice cream. "Jeannie!"

He scooped her into his arms, his un-gloved hand numb. It took some effort to get his fingers to brush the hair away from her face. Blood had frozen where it trickled from her nose. She had the makings of a hell of a shiner under one eye. He tried to feel for a pulse but his hand was dead. He removed his other glove with his teeth and felt around her neck.

There it was. She was alive!

Jeannie groaned, her lips parting slightly.

Holli kept her flashlight trained on the gathering of bat men, Sherm and the creatures that looked to be recovering from their initial trepidation.

Nichols stared at the men who had lost interest in their wounded pet. His eyes flashed with hate.

"You bald freaks!"

A volcano of anger swelled through Nichols. He used his non-frozen left hand and fired into the crowd. Being right handed, his shots went wild, though one caught a man in his stomach. His eyes widened as he stared at the blossoming wound. His knees buckled and he fell onto his side, never once uttering a sound.

Nichols pulled the trigger until the slide locked back on an empty magazine. He looked back at the base, wondering if there was any safe space left for them. It was highly doubtful. What little they could see thanks to their flashlights and headlamps revealed total destruction.

The bat men kept their ground, utterly uninterested in the one Nichols had shot.

He heard scuffling in the snow and whipped around to see Sherm running for the base.

Coward, he seethed. Did he think he was going to be safe in there?

Nichols tensed, rocking Jeannie in his lap. He waited for the inevitable.

"Where are we?"

Jeannie reached up and touched the frozen blood in his beard.

He instantly forgot about everything else. When she tried to push herself up he held her down. "Easy. Easy. Take stock before you rock."

It was what she would always say to him whenever they were out spelunking or white water rafting or on any of their adventures and he'd taken a tumble. Before popping up and declaring himself a-ok, she wanted him to sit back and quietly assess the damage.

Jeannie grimaced, the closest she could get to a grin. She looked around.

"It's so dark and cold. Did we lose power?"

"We're outside, honey."

A flash of shock quickly passed as realization set in. "They came for us."

Nichols nodded. She didn't have a hat or balaclava. He'd have to find one, soon. His own were encased in bloody ice and would only make things worse. The fact that she wasn't shivering worried him.

"We're outside," he said. "They destroyed the base."

"Where are they? Did they leave?"

He tilted her so she could see them when he swept his headlamp in their direction. They gazed at the couple as if they were part of some intriguing science experiment.

"Not good," she said, grimacing as she turned away. She reached up and cradled her head. "One of them kicked me in the head like it was a goddamn football."

Nichols wished there were a way they could tell the bat men apart so he could make tearing its head off his final act. If there was such a thing as karma, the one he'd shot had been Jeannie's aggressor.

Not that he believed in karma. Not now, not here. If karma was real, what in the holy hell had they done in their many lives to deserve this?

"Why are they just standing there?" she asked.

"I think they're content to just watch us freeze to death."

A drop of blood splattered on Jeannie's jacket.

Nichols checked to see if he had a bloody nose. He didn't.

More blood dripped on his wife to the point where he had to pull away.

She pointed at his face. "It's melting."

He wiped his beard, his hand coming away wet and crimson.

How?

The goop from the beast he'd shot left crimson splatter marks in the snow. Nichols flexed the fingers of his exposed hands. The numbness was leaching away.

He looked over at Holli who had removed her hood and hat. "What's happening?" she said.

He didn't have a clue.

"Fuck me sideways," Dallas grumbled. He was on all fours, spitting into the snow. His head swiveled toward Nichols. "They wreck the place?"

"Yeah."

The bat men seemed closer than they had been before. The wind was non-existent, which was rarer than Christmas in July. The temperature was rising fast. Nichols felt himself starting to sweat.

Dallas nudged C-Rod and North until they were awake.

"If we're outside, why do I feel so damn hot?" Dallas said.

Nichols was about to reply when a blood-curdling scream snatched the words from his mouth.

Sherm came bursting from the wrecked base wielding a spear in each hand. He ran the spears into the nearest bat-man, driving it to the ground. He stepped on the man's chest and pulled the spears free, blood hissing in a fountain.

He tossed a spear to Nichols. "Come on!"

The man had come unglued. He was no coward. He was going to die on his own terms.

Holli ran for the spear.

Sherm held his spear like a lance and ran at another of the bat men, a war cry echoing in the night. Before the tip could penetrate the man's chest, two muscular hands grabbed the spear and stopped its forward momentum cold. With a flick of the wrist, the spear was wrested from Sherm's grasp.

Nichols snatched the spear away from Holli.

He hurried to get to Sherm after gently laying Jeannie down.

A pair of bat men had positioned themselves on either side of Sherm, while the one he'd tried to kill snapped the spear, which had been the thick handle of a shovel, as if it were made of straw.

A chorus of roars sounded to Nichols' left.

He had to get to Sherm before it was too late.

CHAPTER TWENTY

Nichols saw C-Rod out of the corner of his eye making a beeline toward Sherm as well. He wasn't sure if it was a suicide mission at this point, but Nichols couldn't just sit back and idly watch his teammate die.

He was only a few feet from Sherm, who now had both his arms in the clutches of the bat men, when his world was suddenly flipped end over end. His lower back throbbed and his headlamp flew off, surrendering him into dizzying pitch-blackness. Was that Jeannie screaming? He was weightless, confused, and blind.

It didn't last long.

Nichols landed on his side, all his breath exploding from his burning lungs. Legs kicking out, he struggled for air. He heard a heavy thud beside him, and felt the presence of something large looming close by, but all that mattered was getting one precious breath.

It mercifully came just as he started to see white sparks exploding in the corners of his eyes. He rolled onto his back, drawing in air greedily, his body aching but muscles relaxing.

Something touched his arm.

"You all right, boss?"

It was C-Rod. He was so close, but Nichols couldn't see a thing.

"No, but I'll live."

When he sat up, ripples of pain shot from his lower back to the base of his skull.

There were more screams.

It was Jeannie.

And Holli.

Dallas and North were shouting as well.

"Where are they?" Nichols said.

C-Rod had a hold on the sleeve of his jacket and wouldn't let go. "I don't know. What the hell happened to us?"

As if in answer, Nichols heard a heavy snort and recoiled at the stench rolling over them.

"I think we got flipped by one of those things."

"Makes sense," C-Rod said. "My legs feel like they got whacked with a Louisville Slugger."

Nichols looked for Holli's flashlight and headlamp. He thought he saw it for a moment but it seemed to hide behind something blacker than the pitch. It was then he realized the light was being blocked by the massive creature standing in front of him.

He got back down on his stomach.

"What are you doing?" C-Rod asked, not relinquishing his grip.

"There they are," he said.

He could see *under* the beast. The only thing illuminated was Sherm. The light bounced all around, as if someone was holding Holli back and she was struggling to break free.

It must have been Dallas.

Jeannie called out for him.

"We're here!" Nichols shouted.

The men who had Sherm so far hadn't done anything. It was as if they were awaiting a command from someone higher up. Whenever Sherm tried to wriggle free, they must have tightened their grip because he would cry out in agony.

"Let's kick their asses," C-Rod said, tugging on Nichols to get up.

The animal standing guard over them roared. C-Rod got back down.

"I don't think it's going to let us," Nichols said. His mind whirred in a million directions. Jeannie had stopped, which meant she must have heard him. How the hell were they going to get to Sherm? And even if they did, what happened next? And why was the temperature rising?

He heard Dallas shout, "I'm coming for you, Sherm."

Sherm shot back, "Don't! Aggghhhh!"

"You see the light?" Nichols whispered to C-Rod.

"Yeah."

"We're going to have to follow it, but to do that, we have to crawl under this thing. And fast."

He hoped it was as blind as they were in the dark but doubted it. This creature didn't survive out here without being able to adjust to the light and temperature changes.

However, there was no other way to get to Sherm…or Jeannie.

"I'll go first," Nichols said. "If it tries to stomp me, use the distraction to run around it and get to the others."

What he didn't tell him was that there may be other animals waiting around to stop them, but that was a bridge they'd burn when they got to it.

"This is insane," C-Rod said.

"Everything is at this point. Now let's go."

He felt the pressure release from his arm and lunged forward, using the slick ground to propel him like when he was a kid and would ski down the reservoir hill on his stomach when it was his brother's turn to use the toboggan.

Miraculously, he made it through unscathed and was up on his feet, once again running toward Sherm. He heard C-Rod cry out in pain behind him. Sherm matched it with his own wail of agony.

C-Rod felt like he'd been dosed with some major acid. How was any of this happening? He liked horror movies as much as the next guy, but he had no desire to live in one.

His body ached in more places than he could count. He'd once been jumped coming out of a bar because he'd made the mistake of buying a drink for a pretty brunette with impressive cleavage that looked to have been there alone. He learned, too late and painfully, that she had been there with her jealous husband and her thug brothers. C-Rod had held his own for a while, but eventually, the four drunk assholes overpowered him. He thought he'd never be as sore as he felt the next day, debating whether or not he should go to the hospital. This had that night beat by a country mile.

And now he had to somehow will his battered body to skate under one of these beasts –a creature he really couldn't even see to judge how he'd make it – and tear ass toward the rest of the crew.

Sure, no problem.

"Fucking white people," he said, spitting into the snow. How many of them surrounded them now? C-Rod liked a good schoolyard scrap, but this was ridiculous. Even if those albino assholes and their ugly monsters suddenly went away, they still had to face the Antarctic winter without shelter.

So, might as well go for broke, son, he thought. *There ain't gonna be a tomorrow to worry about.* There was an odd, unsettling freedom in that.

Nichols had made it through and urged him to follow.

C-Rod lunged ahead in the dark and smashed his face into the hide of one of the creatures, shattering his nose and loosening his front teeth. A massive paw swiped at him, rolling him onto his back. He put his hands up to protect himself. His palms flattening against the underbelly of the beast.

"No!"

The belly slowly descended, intent on crushing him. He put his hands down and rolled to his left. His shoulder smashed into what felt like a brick wall. He quickly rolled to his right, with the same result.

They had boxed him in.

The monster was going to suffocate him.

His claustrophobia took hold of him and roared.

Not like this! Please, not like this!

His legs and arms twisted like a crab in a boiling pot as the beast steadily and inexorably crushed him, his fear only doubling his agony. With a frenzied push, he managed to extricate his upper half from under the creature.

C-Rod screamed, his mind fracturing seconds before his legs.

And suddenly, all of the bat men opened their mouths and started their own supernatural chorus that drowned out all of the screaming and shouting.

The crack of thunder, a near sonic boom unlike any Nichols had ever heard, sent everyone, man and beast alike, to their knees.

CHAPTER TWENTY-ONE

"And then there was light," Jeannie whispered, recalling hot afternoons in summer Bible school.

On the not too distant horizon, the world was on fire. They could feel the heat of it. It melted the snow on the ground and made the layers of clothes around them feel like being encased in hot, wet blankets.

Jeannie tried to blink the tears from her eyes. The sudden brilliance was painful to behold. Her head throbbed.

And in the impossible light, there was silence.

She tried opening her eyes, her thin lids unable to provide adequate shade from the searing light, but it hurt too much. So she kept her face to the ground, using her hands as blinders on either side of her face. Slowly, her eyes began to adjust, but she didn't dare look up.

"Christ, I'm burning up," she heard Dallas say.

"Don't take your coat off," North warned him.

He needn't have said more. As quickly as the light and heat came, it could be replaced by the Pole's regular darkness and icy cold, or worse, in an instant. All the rules had been broken today. There was no telling what was next. What they couldn't be was lulled into thinking the latest development would last.

Where was Rob? Jeannie ached to have him near. He could be right beside her, but there was no way she could look to find him.

"Holli, are you all right?" Jeannie said.

"Aside from feeling like my brain was cut in two and seeing spots with my eyes closed, yeah," she replied. She sounded close.

"Rob?"

There was a long, painful pause. She called for him again.

"I'm here, honey. Keep talking. I'll follow your voice." Thank God he was all right, though not as near as she'd like.

She was at a sudden loss for words when she needed them most. It seemed impossible to come up with something as banal as common blather so her husband could home in on her. Not when they had been overwhelmed by something so inexplicable, there was no word combination that could adequately give voice to it.

"Jean?"

Her lips moved soundlessly.

Think, you idiot, think!

An image came to her, a recollection of a lazy day on her back porch back when she and Rob were first dating. She hadn't thought of it in years. The fact that in her moment of paralysis, this is where her mind would take her made her laugh.

Once her laughter started, she couldn't stop. She must have sounded as if she'd lost her senses.

"I'm coming as fast as I can," Rob said, clearly alarmed.

She took a breath and steadied herself. "You remember the food fight we had?"

"Of course I do. Keep talking."

Jeannie was no longer surrounded by colleagues and bizarre men and terrifying creatures. Across the glaring void, it was just her and Rob, connected by the tether of their voices.

"You looked too peaceful sitting on that beach chair," she continued. "I wanted to do more than sit in the sun. My mother had bought that chocolate cake from Lang's Bakery so we could have it after dinner that night. She knew I hated chocolate cake, but she got it just the same. I was pissed at her and wanted to get you off your ass. Next thing I knew, it was in my hand. Then it was on your face. You sat up so fast, the cake went everywhere. I don't think I'd ever laughed so hard."

"Yeah, until I grabbed a handful and threw it at you," Rob replied, his voice closer.

Jeannie giggled. "You got me right in the chest. Stained my new bikini top. Naturally, I had to return fire."

"And that's where I learned cherry Kool-Aid burns when it gets in your eyes."

"You took the bowl of chips I'd set out and dumped it on my head. So I ran inside and swiped the grapes out of the fruit bowl."

"You had a cannon for an arm, at least in close range with grapes," Rob said.

"Remember all the whipped cream we got on the kitchen floor? And the peanuts and chocolate sauce? When we were done, we both looked at the mess as if someone else had done it."

A hand fell on her shoulder and Rob touched his forehead to hers. "Fastest clean up job of all time."

Jeannie dared to open one eye and was overwhelmed by the increasing brightness. She used her hands to shield both of their eyes now. His skin was so warm, and wet.

"My mother would have killed us," she said.

She bit her lower lip. The word 'killed' shattered the moment, bringing their reality to the fore.

"You're the climatologist," Rob said, knowing her well enough to switch gears. "Any idea what's happening now?"

"Other than the Earth suddenly flipping on its axis, or the sun hurling toward us, I haven't a clue."

"Nothing I like more than consistency." At least he hadn't lost his sarcasm.

No one else spoke a word, all of them enduring the increasing heat and light, trying to ride it out in protective huddles, yet frightened of what would come next. Jeannie was startled when she felt a tap at her back.

"It's just me," Holli said. "I'm melting under all these layers."

They all were. Jeannie's throat was drying up faster than a desert plain in July. She thought of scooping some of the slushy snow into her mouth, but stopped herself when she imagined those creatures stomping around in it, fouling it.

Rob said, "Hey, it's not so bad anymore."

Before Jeannie could open her eyes, he cautioned, "Just take a quick look."

She did. He was right. The light was still as brilliant as a lurking sun, but it had dampened a bit. She tasted sweat as it ran down her face and into her mouth. Rob's breath was hot and sour, with hints of copper from the melting blood in his beard and on his face.

Keeping her eyes on the ground, she found she could open them for longer and longer periods of time before the pain stabbed her in the forehead. It was probably only minutes, but felt like days, before she could keep them open. She didn't dare look up for fear of going blind, but it was an improvement.

She heard North say to Dallas, "This reminds me, you never returned my sunglasses."

Dallas didn't reply.

The bludgeoning heat also began to abate. It was still warm, but not stifling.

The creatures came alive around them, grunting and pawing at the ground. Rob's head pulled away from hers and he said, "Holy crap."

Jeannie pulled her hands away from her face and dared to look around. Her heart tumbled into her stomach.

With the darkness momentarily hastened away, she could plainly see the base for the first time in months. It was utterly and truly demolished. She recalled photos taken of the Amundsen-Scott Base, the memory making her shiver.

But there was worse.

The bat men were legion. Interspersed within their still and silent ranks were beasts of dizzying countenances. She saw what looked to be polar bears, only with horns sprouting from their narrow heads, muzzles black as tar. Penguin-like animals sat on their heavy haunches, their bellies bloated and distended, with massive, misshapen beaks and plumed wings that looked as if they could actually take flight. The thought of those things circling above them terrified her. The penguin things, like the men, were devoid of pigment. If not for their black, blinking eyes, she might have missed them against the alabaster backdrop.

There were other quadrupeds that were just too perplexing to contemplate. They all had two things in common – they were pale, bordering on albino, and menacing.

"You should have saved the bullets," Dallas said. He and North had slowly crept toward them.

She knew what he meant and it pained her. Had they really come to that?

Sherm was still held by two of the men, but he appeared to have passed out. Jeannie saw a tiny tendril of steam escape his mouth.

When her eyes alighted on C-Rod, she gasped. Rob turned to where she was looking and bolted.

C-Rod's left leg was pinned by one of the chimeras. The ground was splattered with blood as it exploded from the pressure. His leg from the knee down was flat, like a deflated balloon.

And somehow he was still conscious.

Dallas ran after Rob, followed by Holli, all three hollering at the animal in an attempt to at least get it to move off of C-Rod.

The beast lowered its head and glowered at them, dark lips pulled back, jagged teeth flashing. Jeannie wanted to help, but the moment she went to stand, she fell back down. She was sure she had a concussion, her stability severely limited. North held onto her.

"They should let him be," he said. "What do they think they can do against that monster?"

"Rob could never."

It would end horribly. Jeannie forced herself to watch. She owed being a witness to his death to her husband. She was sure she wouldn't have to live with it for long before joining him.

CHAPTER TWENTY-TWO

Nichols had no clue what he was going to do to get the creature to step off of C-Rod. It did not look the least bit frightened of their screams and wild gesticulations. This was not some house cat or a raccoon in the yard.

C-Rod looked up and their eyes met. Despite what must be excruciating pain, C-Rod shook his head, asking them to stop.

With a sudden lunge, C-Rod sat up and grabbed the creature by the nose. He'd taken his gloves off, his fingers digging into the dripping, black organ. It howled, rearing back, releasing C-Rod's leg. Rob's gorge lodged in his throat. C-Rod's leg was essentially gone. What was left in its place no more resembled a leg than an ear or a kidney.

"How do you like that, asshole?" C-Rod shouted. He held onto the creature's nose for all he was worth. It lifted him off the ground, his shattered leg flopping, spraying blood and bits of bone. He punched at its eye with his other hand, cursing with anger and defiance.

The closest bat men looked on with indifference.

Oddly enough, C-Rod seemed to be winning the battle. Nichols heard the eyeball pop, saw the viscera come tumbling out in a waterfall. The beast snapped its head and C-Rod was airborne. He landed by Nichols' feet, nearly knocking him down as if he were a bowling pin.

Holli was already taking off her Big Red and pulling off a sweater. She used it to tie a tight knot around his thigh.

Nichols watched from a safe distance as the creature bashed two of the bat men, its blind agony sending it into a desperate gallop. The men's bodies snapped in half like dry timber, their black eyes staring at the bright sky.

"I don't think that's gonna help much," C-Rod said, staring at the makeshift tourniquet. He was panting hard, his complexion like wax.

"It'll stop you from bleeding to death, you dummy," Holli said.

His eyes fluttered. "I think…I think that ship has sailed, Hols."

One of the bat men suddenly sprang toward C-Rod. Nichols darted between them, blocking the man from getting to him. His skin was cold, the muscles underneath hard as stone. They landed in a pile, Nichols on top. The man's mouth opened in a silent scream. His gums were gray and withered, the stench coming from his bowels horrid enough to make Nichols lightheaded. He reared back to deliver one hell of a haymaker to the man's nose when he was tackled, rolling into C-Rod who wailed in agony.

Nichols tried to get up, but he was swarmed by bat men. They pinned him to the ground. He was just able to turn his head to see them do the same to Dallas and Holli. It was like being buried under steel beams. He couldn't so much as squirm under their powerful weight. It was getting harder to breathe.

"Get the fuck off me!" C-Rod shouted.

One of the bat men crouched by his squashed leg. It grabbed his coat and pulled him closer. C-Rod kicked at him with his good leg, his boot bouncing harmlessly off the thing's mid-section.

Two other bat men scampered forward to hold C-Rod's shoulders down.

The bat-man used one hand to tear C-Rod's pants free, exposing smashed muscles and bone. The thing got down on its belly and latched its mouth onto the stub of C-Rod's knee.

"What the fuck are you doing?" C-Rod screamed, writhing to pull away.

It slurped hungrily at his leg. Nichols watched in revulsion as its throat pulsed with each draught of C-rod's blood. Another bat-man came and joined in suckling on C-rod's leg.

"Get the hell off of him!" Holli shouted from under the pile of bat men.

C-Rod's protests turned to sobs as helplessness set in.

"Get off me, you fucking freaks," he blubbered. "Get off my fucking…gahhhhhh!"

His eyes rolled up in his head and his chest heaved once…twice…slowly settling down after the third breath and rising no more. Holli's scream was heartbreaking.

When it was done, the men stepped away, allowing Nichols, Holli and Dallas to stand.

The husk of C-Rod lay on the floor, cooling.

Blood ran down the chins and chests of the two bat men who had feasted on him.

Dallas lunged for one of them, catching it at the knees and pile driving it to the ground. He hammered blow after blow to its face, snapping its neck left and right.

Nichols made to do the same to the other one when Jeannie's voice stopped him cold.

He looked over to see four bat men had hold of her, one for each limb.

The bloody bat-man gave something resembling a sick, evil smile.

"Dallas, stop!" Nichols shouted.

His maintenance manager kept pummeling the bat-man.

"Dallas!"

With his fist raised, Dallas paused. He craned his neck to see Jeannie in the clutches of the men. North lay face down on the ground, a foot planted on the back of his neck.

The men took a half-step away from Jeannie, keeping their hold on her legs and arms, eliciting a fresh cry of pain.

Dallas rolled off the man.

"Get your hands off of her," Nichols warned the bat men. He took slow but steady strides toward his wife.

"Oh God, help me!" Jeannie wailed. Tears streamed down her face, a face that was locked in a rictus of unbridled agony.

"I said put her the fuck down!" Nichols trumpeted. He was angry and terrified, his body gone numb, the edges of his vision going black. It felt as if he were watching himself from above. They had his wife.

They had his wife!!!

He would tear them apart with his bare hands if he had to.

Jeannie's cries escalated to a fever pitch as they tugged on her limbs. Nichols thought he heard the wet thump of her bones slipping from their sockets.

He started to run, his hands balled into fists.

Wrapped in his rage, he didn't hear the creature galloping to intercept him. One second, Nichols was locked on his wife and her tormentors, the next, he ran into the foul-smelling hide of a hairless creature, a bat-man riding on its back.

This man was different than the others.

He was bigger. Much bigger. He had to be at least eight feet tall with thick, powerful limbs, his head more conical than the others. He stared at Nichols from atop his mount, the sickening beast looking like a cross between a walrus and a horse, only double the size of each.

The man jumped from its back and grabbed Nichols by the throat, lifting him off the ground. He tried to punch himself free, but his reach wasn't long enough to connect.

He was carried, his feet inches from the ground, his breath all but gone, around the creature so he could once again witness Jeannie's torture.

"Watch," the man said in Rob's ear, his voice older than time, a deep rumble from the pits of hell.

He can talk!

Nichols couldn't even call out to his wife.

"Rob, help me, please!" she screamed.

The bat men dug their heels and pulled as one.

Jeannie's limbs pulled away with a tearing that echoed across the shattered base. Blood spurted from the four vicious wounds. Her torso flopped onto the ground, twitching as if an electric current was running through her.

Rob's mind spun like a top.

There were voices, but he couldn't focus on them.

He watched Jeannie twitch for several more seconds before going still. The bat men licked at the ragged ends of her arms and legs, sucking on them like children with a snow cone.

Dozens of shadows flittered on the ground. Nichol's rolled his eyes upward as his lungs begged for breath and his mind wished for revenge and a swift death. He watched in horror as a flock of birds that may have at one time been albatross but had been disfigured to a more vulture-like countenance descended on Jeannie's body. They pecked at her with savage fury, tearing away at her clothes, casting aside the bits of cloth and insulation. They ate her eyes, lips and nose, heads craning back to swallow each morsel. They dug into her chest and stomach, searching for food, steam roiling from her open corpse as if it were an open manhole.

Rob, his own eyes popping from his skull, saw it all.

CHAPTER TWENTY-THREE

Dallas saw the light go from Jeannie's eyes the instant she was quartered. Moments later, he saw the same with Rob Nichols. He was sick to his stomach. He'd seen terrible things in combat, things that he'd spent the past two decades trying to forget. No matter how hard he tried, one particular day always clawed its way back into his brain, haunting him more than any vengeful ghost. He hadn't told anyone, but he often prayed that he would get Alzheimer's or suffer a debilitating stroke, anything to finally carve that malignancy from his brain. He thought he would never, ever see anything worse. He'd been dead wrong. Poor Jeannie, she had probably never hurt anyone in her too-short life. If these men from nowhere did that to her, what was in store for the rest of them?

The bizarre birds squawked angrily as they tore at Jeannie's remains. Dallas couldn't bear it any longer. Holli wept somewhere close to him. The giant bat-man let Nichols fall to the floor where he crumpled in a heaving heap. Nichols let out a lone, long, keening wail that made Dallas breakout in goosebumps.

All was lost. There was no one on this continent that could save them. He wasn't sure the army could do much against these men and their hideous beasts.

The weight was suddenly lifted from his body. He pushed himself up on his elbows, looking back at the men who had pinned him down. They were no longer interested in him, their big black eyes trained on the larger man who had held Nichols by the throat.

"Take them!" the man said.

Dallas was roughly picked up by two men. Their grip conveyed that he was not to resist. The pain of their vice-like hands didn't register. He was too taken aback by the fact that this man who did not appear to be a man at all could speak! And speak English, of all things.

He was beginning to think he imagined it when the man approached Sherm's limp body held up by a pair of men and said, "Let me see."

One of the men grabbed Sherm's hood and pulled his head up.

The large man bent to look at Sherm's face. His head tilted from side to side, studying the unconscious seismologist. He straightened and waved one of his enormous hands. The men hauled Sherm away, depositing him on the back of one of the creatures. It grunted, and then started to walk in its lumbering gait.

"Where are you taking him?" Dallas asked.

The large man looked at him and narrowed his oversized eyes. "Taking *you*."

Nichols was lifted off the ground as if he were a rag doll. He didn't protest when he was thrown onto the back of a rank-smelling animal. It looked like a cross between a yak and walrus, huge tusks weighing its head down.

Holli, on the other hand, fought wildly against the men who held her.

"No, no, no, no!" she screamed. "I'm not going anywhere with you!"

"Hols, you need to calm down," Dallas said. He was pushed into the hide of an animal and held there for a moment. Their eyes met. "Live to fight another day."

It didn't stop her completely, but she did settle down a bit. He didn't want the men to perceive her as too much trouble and dispatch her the way they had Jeannie. He'd seen enough death for one day. He could only hope that his own came before anyone else's.

He, North and Holli were loaded onto the creatures, each surrounded by men who would surely beat them to within an inch of their lives if they tried to jump off.

"You don't have to worry," Dallas said as they started to move. He had to latch onto a tuft of coarse hair so he didn't fall off. "We got nowhere to run to."

The lesser bat men paid him no mind. He twisted around to look for their leader. "Even you have to understand that. Big head means big brain, right?"

"Quiet," the man rumbled.

"Fuck you," Holli spat.

The creature carrying North came up beside Dallas. This beast resembled a mangy polar bear with patches of raw flesh that looked close to bleeding. He looked at the beaten and weary doctor. He saw the heavy fog misting from North's mouth. The temperature was dropping. That was not good. They were all sweating bullets. Once the beyond bitter cold returned, they would freeze to death, encased in their own ice.

"How long you think we got, doc?"

North stared at him with bloodshot eyes. "Until they decide they want to pull one of us to ribbons?"

"I'm talking about the cold. Can't you feel it's coming back?"

"If we're lucky, not long. But I'm not feeling very lucky at the moment."

Holli hurled another slew of invectives at the leader and her animal was punched on the hide by the bat men, spurring it to trot away from them.

For some reason, the five of them had been chosen to be taken…where? He had to admit, a part of him was curious to see where these men and creatures came from.

Above them, strange birds swooped and circled. It was as if every living thing down here followed the commands of the giant man. Dallas used to like to listen to the old Art Bell radio show, the one that dealt with things like UFOs, ghosts, government conspiracies and all things paranormal and strange. He recalled a show about the cover-up of the discovery of giant human skeletons, many of them found in the nineteenth century. Men and women as big as fifteen feet in height were unearthed all across America and other countries as well. The story went that all of the bones were either destroyed or snatched up by the Smithsonian, where they were buried deep in their vaults, never to see the light of day. The history of man was controlled by organizations like the Smithsonian with their own singular agendas.

At the time, Dallas had thought it amusing yet utter nonsense. If the bones of giants had truly been found in so many places, at least one of the skeletons would have made it to the public.

Now, he wasn't so sure.

One thing he was positive of – this leader was no one to mess with. You didn't command man and beast alike through song and praise. No, they feared him. So did Dallas.

They traveled toward the light on the horizon. A few times, Dallas had noticed that it had started to flicker, just faintly, but enough to tell him it might not last.

"Wandering in the desert," North mumbled.

"What's that?" Dallas said.

"You think there's a Promised Land out there where the light is coming from?"

"If what's gone on here is any indication, I think it's a land that promises to be fucking bizarre."

"And deadly." North took a deep, shuddering breath. "You know, I came down here to die."

"You're just in shock. You're the doc. You came here to stop other people from dying."

North cast a quick glance behind them, where Jeannie and C-Rod's bodies lay. "A lot of good I've done. But that's not it. I chose this place because I knew it could be dangerous. I've wanted to die for a long time now. I just haven't had the guts to outright kill myself. I was beginning to think I'd pussied out yet again, choosing a pretty damn safe station, albeit it in a treacherous location. But now that death is here, I don't think I'm ready to face it. I was always so sure that my wife was out there, waiting for me. If these things can exist," he swept his hand across the great expanse of marching men and animals, "can anything we've been taught be true? If we have no clue what lives in our world, how can we even presume to know what's waiting for us in the next?"

Dallas side-eyed the giant to see if the alien man was listening. Hell, his ears were big enough to hear a conversation all the way in Argentina. The giant seemed to pay them no mind.

"I don't know what to tell you about the afterlife," Dallas said. "I never was one for Heaven or Hell or that place in between. I always saw death as a mercy. You flip the switch and it's lights out. No more pain. No more worries. No more writing checks out to the goddamn IRS. I am glad you don't want to die, doc. You fight it when it comes, and it might come soon. If we're gonna die, we need to take as many of these albino eggheads with us as possible."

North nodded and a faint smile played on his face. "Albino eggheads. I like it."

"Kinda makes them seem less imposing if you give them a funny name. I'd tell you all the names I gave the Iraqis back in Desert Storm, but that's one of those *you have to have been there* kind of things to properly understand."

Dallas looked over at Nichols, his zombie stare locked on the horizon and someplace beyond it. He said, "Nichols, you hear me?"

The man didn't so much as shift his eyes. He was gone. Dallas couldn't blame him. If he'd watched his wife get ripped apart like that, he was sure his mind would have shattered in as many pieces or more.

"Shock," North said.

"You think he'll come out of it?"

North considered it for a moment. "Only if he wants to."

A snippet of Holli's curses came floating back to them on the soft blowing wind.

There was nothing more to say. They rocked on the backs of the beasts, waiting to see what fresh hell awaited them.

They didn't have to wait long.

CHAPTER TWENTY-FOUR

Holli was blind with anger, electric with fear. She knew yelling at their captors was next to useless, but she had to do something to vent it all out before the top of her head exploded. The army of bat men had separated her from everyone else for her efforts, but she didn't care. It's not as if they were being carted to some five-star resort.

What they'd done to Jeannie and C-Rod!

It was more than she could handle, and Holli had shouldered her share of heavy burdens.

Several times she'd tried to leap off the horrendous smelling creature, but each time the guards positioned around it pushed her back up with hands that felt as if their bones were made of iron.

What she hoped was to garner the full attention of their leader. Even if it was just to command her to shut the hell up, she could use that as an opportunity to open some kind of dialogue. There were nights when her mother was out either with friends or late at work when her piece of shit stepfather, stinking of beer and pork rinds, would come to her room. The fever to touch her burned in his eyes like campfires. Sometimes – not often enough for her to retain any sense of normalcy or innocence – she would get him to talk. Not casually discussing the weather. No, that would not have made her soul feel so used and tattered.

She'd learned he liked dirty talk. So much so that with a few words, she could get him to finish before he even started. It sickened her to say the words, but those same vile words saved her from physical violation…occasionally.

Holli was sure any conversation with the giant man would be this side of terrifying. Even the timbre of his voice made her weak. But if talking could somehow gain her an edge, she would do it.

"Where's your limp dick boss?" she shouted, casting about for the king of the bat men. All she saw were identical minions and the strange array of animals. "Is he afraid of a woman? Is that why he had Jeannie killed? Scared we'll ruin your little sausage party?"

Even Holli knew she sounded ridiculous, but who really cared?

"Maybe one of you – "

The rest of the words died in her throat.

As if popping up from nowhere, cloaked in silence, a valley of huge ice spires jutting from the frozen tundra came into view. Dozens and dozens of the gargantuan spikes pointed this way and that, forming a disorienting latticework of ice and snow.

She couldn't help thinking of Superman's Fortress of Solitude.

Only she didn't think there would be any bit of peaceful seclusion there.

The powerful light that had chased away the gloom of the South Pole's landscape emanated from the center of the ice spires. A beam of brilliance shot straight into the clouded atmosphere, reflecting back down to the snow-covered ground.

Holli clasped her hand over her mouth.

The earthquake.

Sherm had said the epicenter was close.

This must have been the source. It had felt and sounded like the earth itself was exploding. She had flown over this area before landing on the strip alongside Freedom Base. These towers of ice had not been there then. If they had, they would have been the center of all of their studies.

Even though she was just a maintenance tech, she didn't need a doctorate to connect the dots. The earthquake must have been the impetus to free the incredible filigree of ice from below the surface. That breach had given free passage to the bizarre men and beasts that were herding them to the eye of the storm. But how had they been living under the ice? The question was moot. They were here and they were real.

The false sun glinted off the far-reaching ice steeples. Holli thought she saw innumerable shapes moving about the base of the structure.

For once, Holli was at a loss for words.

She wished C-Rod was here beside her. For all the complaining she did over his immature, boorish behavior, deep down, she liked him like an annoying brother. He'd have the perfect, inappropriate thing to say right now. She didn't think she'd ever get over his death. Her only solace was that she was damn sure she wouldn't live with the image for long.

The bat men let out a piercing cry in chilling harmony. Holli watched the distant shapes scramble, disappearing under the ice spires.

What's beneath all that? she thought.

Resigned to her fate, Holli sat in uncomfortable silence. One of the strange birds swooped over her head, just missing getting tangled in her hair.

It was a good reminder that she needed to put her hood and hat back on. The temporary rise in temperature was rapidly bleeding away. Her lips were chapped to the point of cracking and bleeding. Her mouth was assaulted by the acrid taste of old pennies.

The belly of the beast.

The phrase looped through her head. They were being escorted to the belly of the beast, only this beast was so foreign to her, to all of them, she had no clear footing to stand on.

It took the better part of half an hour to make it to the base of what she'd deemed the *ice castle*. Only this castle was so massive, so far-reaching, it made her nauseous to even try to visually take it all in.

Consignment to her fate finally loosened her tongue. "This where you freaks live?"

One of the bat men looked up at her, his ebony eyes utterly unreadable.

"Looks about as cozy as an outhouse on a frozen lake."

Again, no reaction. She was sure they couldn't understand her. There was always the hope that they had a concept of sarcasm. A distant hope.

"Will you look at that."

North's voice took her by surprise. He and Dallas were to her right, staring in wild-eyed wonder at the city of ice. Nichols trotted up to her left on the back of one of the beasts, silent and broken.

"You think they're having us over for a five course dinner and a tour of the whatever you call it down there?" Holli asked, less than earnest.

"Only if we were trapped in a H.G. Wells novel," North replied. "I don't think our hosts will be quite so aristocratic."

Holli shivered. "It's getting cold again."

Dallas pointed at the shaft of light. "It's starting to dim."

He was right. Whatever gasses were released from the earthquake – if that's what caused the powerful light – were dissipating. Sooner than they'd prefer, they'd be in the dark and freezing their asses off.

Holli had no intention of freezing to death. If she was going to punch out, she wanted it to be much grander than that.

As they got closer to the ice city, she made up her mind.

"I can't just sit here and let them feed me to some crazy animal or worse," she said to Dallas and North.

"What could be worse?" Dallas said.

"Them," she replied icily, pointing at the bat men. As far as she'd seen, there were no women about. They had all the workings of a normal man, left out in plain sight. What if they decided to use the weapons between their legs against her? She knew for sure that she wouldn't be able to endure it. Her stepfather had seen to that.

"I'm outta here," she said, raising her heels under her buttocks.

"Wait," Dallas said. "Don't do anything crazy."

She gave her boss a wink. "Too late for that."

In one swift motion, she stood on the back of the beast and ran along its spine, past the top of its head and down its long, narrow snout. It jerked its head and tried to snap at her, but she was already airborne, arms pinwheeling as she free-fell into the snow ahead of the creature. The impact sent shivers of pain up her legs and into her hips. Holli rolled on the ground, letting the rest of her body in motion distribute the impact.

The men around the beast set after her, but she was already on her feet, legs pumping furiously, heading west of the ice city. Ahead of her were rows of more men and their freakish pets, but so what? She wasn't going to stop until *they* stopped her.

Dallas and North cried out for her to come back, but she was past rational thought. She wanted one of the creatures to stomp her like they'd done C-Rod or bite her head off. Anything was better than being left a plaything for the bat men.

Tears stung her eyes. She ran as fast as she could under several layers of pants. It was never going to be fast enough.

The men parted, making way for her as the waters before Noah.

Why?

Just keep running, she demanded of herself.

The plain before her was flat and dead, offering no cover, no safe place to hide. She would run until her legs gave out, until her heart exploded. There was fat chance of that. Holli never thought she'd regret all the hours in the gym. If anything, her legs and side would cramp. That would halt her escape. She'd be left paralyzed and useless in the snow. Her heart would palpitate wildly, but it would not stop, would not erupt. Her treacherous, traitorous heart would leave her to endure the pain and humiliation.

Something galloped heavily behind her. She didn't dare look back.

Holli knew what was coming.

The giant leader and his twisted steed were closing in on her. The back of her neck prickled, anticipating the giant's touch.

He snatched onto her hood, yanking her off the ground, her legs moving as if still tethered to the ground. Her view of the world shifted, swinging crazily from the horizon to the illuminated sky, to the hard, unreadable face of the muscular leader. The beast didn't break stride as she was carried aloft, hanging by the hood of her Big Red.

"Just fucking kill me!" she spat in the giant's face.

His eyes were so black, it was like looking into the empty mouth of an endless cave. Nothing reflected back to her. Nothing human, at least.

Holli lashed out with her boot, connecting with his nose. There was no crack of cartilage. He didn't even blink. A painful reverberation ran up her leg and into her teeth.

She kicked with her other leg, but the giant caught her by the ankle before she could connect. His grip tightened, harder and harder, until she thought her ankle bone would turn to powder. No matter the pain, she refused to cry out. They stared at one another, the wind whipping past them as they hurtled toward the ice castle.

"Get your freak hands off me," she hissed, her teeth grinding so hard she knew they would start to chip any second now.

Her body swayed back and forth to the undulating rhythm of the creature. She had to stop the pain. Her foot had gone numb.

Holli reared back to punch the giant.

He released her ankle, her relief existing for the beat of a bird's flapping wing. The giant punched her so hard, her head snapped back. She heard the crack more than felt it, a split-second before her world went mercifully black.

CHAPTER TWENTY-FIVE

As terrifying as everything was, a small part of North couldn't help marveling at the natural-yet-unnatural structure before them. He'd grown up on a steady diet of movies like *Journey to the Center of the Earth, At the Earth's Core* and *The Land That Time Forgot*. For a spell when he was ten, he told everyone he was going to be Doug McClure when he grew up.

You got your wish, he thought.

Except these weren't cheap special effects and they didn't have a prissy Englishman as comic relief.

He should be too scared to think straight, but as they stopped at the foot of the monumental ice structure, he could only stare up to the tips of the spires, then back down at the strange gathering of man and monster, and feel his chest and head bursting with strange wonder.

"You ever even imagine anything like it? It's…it's beautiful," he said, his voice hushed to a whisper as if he were in church.

"Have you lost your mind, doc?" Dallas shot back.

North slowly nodded. "I may have, Dallas. I wouldn't rule that out. No sir, I wouldn't rule it out."

The returning army was greeted by even more of the identical men. They came streaming out of the various odd geometric breaks in the ice. With them came a menagerie of pale skinned and furred creatures of indeterminate origin. Some – the ones that circled around the bat men's legs – appeared to be a variation of domestic pets. They were short, four-legged, with long, ragged ropes of fur. They had the long, drooping snouts of aardvarks with pink, active eyes.

A completely hairless animal that he could only think of as a mule walked past, its back loaded with sacks made of some type of reed or weed he couldn't identify. It had no ears or tail, but its legs were thick and sturdy, designed to cart heavy weights. Its back was bowed. North didn't realize he was reaching out to touch it as it lumbered by until Dallas shouted, "Don't do that!"

"All this time, beneath our feet, there was a whole word," North said. The bat men surrounded them, though there wasn't a trace of curiosity on their stone faces.

"Yeah, but a world of what?" Dallas eyed the men coolly as if taking each one's measure to exact revenge at a later date.

"I don't know," North said.

A chevron of alabaster birds angled between two of the ice spires. Their long, heron-like legs fanned out behind them.

"North."

"Shhh. Just be quiet. Take it in."

It was like stepping onto an alien world. North didn't know…couldn't know the intentions of the members of this newfound race. Yes, their actions had been violent and swift. But did that make them violent by nature? There was no way to know without an understanding of who or what they were. North felt it in his gut that they had to remove their all too human perceptions from the equation from here on in. As the Buddhists would say, they had to live in the moment, free from judgment and emotion.

There was no point telling Dallas this. He wouldn't understand. North could hear him grumbling but had tuned out his words. Words would get in the way.

One of the bat men slapped the hide of the animal North sat upon and it began moving again, deeper into the city of ice.

As they slipped under the cathedral-like entrance, he could hear Holli's protestations echoing within the icy walls. What he saw next took his breath away.

"Will you look at that," Dallas croaked.

They entered what North guessed would pass for a town square. Within the wide open space mingled more of the bizarre men (yet no women), silently exchanging depthless glances. In the center of the square was a burbling fountain, the waters red as fresh drawn blood. The crimson water splashed onto the icy floor, staining it so it reminded him of the cherry snow cones he loved when he was a child.

The closer they got to the fountain, the deeper the mineral tang to the air.

"It's like the Blood Falls," North said.

"Blood Falls?"

He looked at Dallas, for the first time taking his eyes off the dizzying spectacle. "You never heard of them? It's an actual red waterfall spilling out of the Taylor Glacier. They say it comes from a lake, buried deep under the ice millions of years ago. The high salt content kept the water from freezing, and the higher levels of iron have turned it red." A light splash of water touched North's face. The water was so cold, it felt like getting hit by pebbles. "They say watching the Blood Falls is like looking at the rushing waters from Hell itself. I'm not a religious man, so I wouldn't go that far, but looking at this, I can see how it would touch people's deepest fears."

He wiped at the crimson water fleck on his face with his finger. When Dallas turned away, he touched his finger to the tip of his tongue. What was it? It certainly wasn't water.

Dallas shook his head. "You think this is coming from the same lake?"

"I don't know. I'd believe anything just about now."

The beast shied away from the cold spray, trotting past it. North wished he could slow it down. He wanted to dismount and put his hand in the fountain, to taste the water.

Maybe Dallas was right and he had gone over the bend.

He looked back at Nichols who didn't even so much as flick a glance at the red fountain. His eyes were downcast, fixed on a place that was far, far from here.

Many of the bat men had lined up on each side of the prisoner procession. They were rapidly approaching a tunnel of ice that appeared to open into a massive chamber. North speculated about what they could possibly be witness to next.

He didn't have long to wonder.

CHAPTER TWENTY-SIX

Sherm awoke in agony. Every joint in his body felt as if it had been dislocated and roughly jammed back in. His ribs and head pounded. His vision was blurry. The air smelled funny.

Opening his eyes, he panicked, thinking for a brief flash that he was blind. Jerking his head sideways, he realized he had instead been face down on what felt like a rug.

Where was he?

What had happened?

He strained to remember, but his brain was wrapped in fog and forgetfulness.

Someone was shouting. Sherm caught snatches of choice curses. It was a woman. A woman in great distress.

Holli!

Sherm pushed himself up, and when he did, he wished he were back in the comforting black of unconsciousness.

Eyes casting about, searching for Holli, everything came rushing back, his mind reeling from the influx of new, startling images, scents and sounds. He'd been draped across the back of one of those strange animals, its funk making his nose hairs curl. He turned his face away from its ropy hide, his nostrils opening wide, taking in the metallic air that filled this…this what? It looked as if he was inside a skyscraper made of ice.

The second he moved to get off the creature, he was pushed back on by rough hands. The men with their giant ebony eyes stared up at him.

"Holli!" he croaked, his aching ribs making it hard to shout.

"Sherm! Are you all right?"

It was Dallas from somewhere behind him. He looked back to find the maintenance manager riding beside North, with Nichols looking lost and beaten a few paces behind them. "No, I'm not," he replied, the cloud of smoke his breath created forming a wall of gauze, distorting his vision. "Where the hell are we?"

Dallas and North stared ahead, unwilling or unable to reply.

Sherm followed their gaze.

Oh shit.

Within the cavernous framework of towering ice lay a type of cave opening. It was tall and wide and as pitch black as the eyes of the men that had captured them. To the side of the opening lay a tumble of boulders made of ice. Sitting atop the scree was a man that looked like the others but was twice their size. He held Holli's arms behind her back with one hand, her struggles failing to make the muscles in his arm even twitch. Their eyes met and she slumped back onto a sharp block of ice.

When they were close enough to speak without having to shout, Sherm said, "Are you hurt?"

She shook her head.

A warmer current of air trickled out of the cave. The cave terrified Sherm more than the bat men.

"Where are we?"

Holli tugged against her captor, the giant looking elsewhere, as if not concerned about them in the least. "I'm thinking home sweet home for these freaks. Or at least the front porch." She nodded at the cave. "If you ask me, home is down there."

Sherm took a moment to study the walls of ice around and above them. The layers of various discoloration told him this was centuries of buried ice, freshly exposed. This hadn't been here when he first arrived. It would have been impossible to miss from the air. This was fresh which could only mean it had been given rise by the earthquake. These massive pillars of ancient ice had somehow pushed their way through to the surface. Even more impossible, they had assembled themselves to form what could easily be interpreted as manmade formations.

Had all of this always been here, a city in full, populated by strange life forms in the most inhospitable land on the planet, deep under the surface? It was preposterous, yet it was here.

The air emanating from the cave felt just warm enough to support life. It wasn't warm, but it wasn't the kind of cold that brought only death.

Their world had been thrust upon Sherm's, spitting up like lava. They were as unprepared and possibly confused and confounded as the crew of Freedom Base. But what the bat men had over them was sheer strength and numbers. Here Sherm thought man was just in the learning stages of how to one day conquer the Antarctic, when the truth was, they were never going to be the alpha. It had already been done by a race that was, at least physically, far superior.

Being a scientist himself, it dawned on him why the men hadn't simply wiped them all out back at the base.

Sherm and his companions were being brought to their world as a curiosity. And what did you do with curiosities?

You studied them. Sometimes, you did so in terrible, horrible ways.

Fear of death by freezing was one thing. What potentially waited for them at the bottom of that cavern nearly stopped Sherm's heart from beating. Worst still, he would die an un-mourned man. He'd grown up in a succession of foster homes, immersing himself in school and studies once he was mercifully old enough to be on his own. There was no special woman waiting for him back home. No close friends. Just a smattering of acquaintances who would mark his loss with a sliver of reflection before moving on and resuming their normal lives.

"We can't let them take us down there," Sherm said.

"You have a submachine gun with endless rounds in your pocket?" Holli replied. This time, when she tugged on her captor, the giant slowly craned its head to peer at her. She dared to look into his eyes for the briefest of moments before whipping her face away in self-preservation.

Sherm barked, "Hey!"

The giant turned to him. Sherm felt as if he were going to fall into the void of its soulless eyes. Despite the crawling fear that scratched up his spine, he refused to break away, searching for something, anything he could latch onto. There was intelligence there, there just had to be, but those portals revealed nothing but the cold, emptiness of death. Sherm knew in that instant there would be no compassion toward them. The scant space between them may have been as wide as the gulf that bridged galaxies. Here were two species very much of this world, though so many worlds apart, it was too daunting to even begin to calculate.

Sherm wanted to escape the awful tractor beam of the giant's steady glaring, but he felt immobilized, his brain and body gone numb.

"Sherm. Sherm!"

Dallas called to him from miles away.

Sherm wanted to speak, but his lower jaw merely fell open like Marley's ghost.

"Sherm!" Then a moment of pressure on his arm. Yes, he felt that! His vision wavered under the shimmer of unbidden tears. *Look away, damn you*!

The pressure came again, followed by a heavy grunt and the sounds of a struggle.

He was saved by something as mundane as a blink, the cold air frosting his tears. Sherm looked over to see Dallas kicking at the bat men who were punishing him for daring to reach out to him.

"Leave him be," Sherm said, reaching across and swatting at the arms of the so-called men battering Dallas. One of them punched Sherm in the side. It felt as if his kidney had been ruptured. The grip of pain that squeezed his back took his breath away.

"Everyone stop!" North shouted at the top of his lungs. To Sherm's amazement, it brought an end to the melee. The doctor had a strange glint in his eye. He pointed at the mouth of the cave. "Looks like our new escorts are coming."

The inky blackness was now flickering with sparkles of encroaching white. It was as if a tornado of lit candles were spinning its way to the surface.

The giant rose to his feet, lifting Holli into the air, her legs kicking futilely.

"They're birds," Dallas said.

Not just any birds. They glowed with their own internal fire. The size of seagulls, the luminous birds spilled out of the cave. They did so as silently as the bat men, their wings extended, not flapping, but riding the warmer current coming from the depths. They did not chitter, they did not squawk.

But they did light up the cave as if daylight had descended. Sherm saw that it sloped downward, the floor a smooth sheet of ice. He was past wondering how birds could glow like lightning bugs stuck in a permanent on-position. Part of him was grateful for their presence. The thought of going into that cave in utter pitch had pricked all of his childhood fears and gave them life into the cowering adult he had become. At least there would be light. He would see sights no man had ever dreamed.

And he would face his death when it came.

The giant straddled one of the beasts, Holli still in his grip, and urged it into the cave. To Sherm's surprise, it didn't zip down the steep ramp like a child on a slide. He noticed the sharp claws that had extended from its paws, each talon finding purchase in the ice. The luminescent birds circled overhead, lighting the way.

"Fascinating," North said, his face lit up with wonder. Even Dallas looked around them in awe. Only Holli and Nichols weren't cowed by the spectacle – the former blinded by anger and desperation, the latter rendered nearly comatose.

The path down into the cave was wide enough to accommodate two tanks, side by side. They marched down and down, this unlikely silent parade of mixed species, the air still crisp but no longer feeling as if it would fill their veins with ice, the passage twinkling with lights from the flitting preternatural birds. Sherm tried in vain to steady his breathing, unable to wipe clear the feeling they were being led down death row.

CHAPTER TWENTY-SEVEN

Eventually, the fight bled out of Holli. Her anger still boiled deep within her, but she no longer had the physical stamina to lash out at her captor. The giant held her aloft as they made their way down the wide tunnel. Her body was exhausted but her mind was still a beehive of thoughts and emotions.

She kept trying to think of lost Antarctic expeditions from the past. There had been several in the hundred years that man had been making the trek, Shackleton's doomed trip being the most famous. As crazy as it sounded, she couldn't stop wondering if these men were somehow descended from a lost band of pioneers. But then how would that explain their identical nature? That could only come about from advanced cloning in a laboratory, and those were leaps in cloning that were, as far as she knew, above and beyond what modern science could accomplish.

And even if she could grasp at a straw to explain the existence of the bat men, how on Earth did these bizarre animals factor in to everything?

"Nazis," she shouted, her voice echoing in the tunnel.

"What did you say?" North replied. He was only a few feet behind, his head swiveling like crazy on his neck as he struggled to take everything in.

"Nazis, of course," she said, chuckling. *Oh boy,* she thought, *laughing at a moment like this is a sure sign you're losing it, girl.* "Weren't the Nazis conducting strange experiments down here during the war? Maybe the whole thing got swallowed up in an earthquake, somehow found a pocket of air and water to survive, and now it's all been regurgitated by Mother Nature." She remembered C-Rod joking about secret Nazi camps and making fun of him for being so stupid. "If C-Rod were here, he'd agree with me."

North looked at her with pity. "No, Hols, I don't think this is leftovers from the Nazis. If they could accomplish this, we'd all be speaking German today."

She shrugged her shoulders, her body dangling in the air. "Then I give up."

"No sense even trying," North said. "Right now, all we can do is observe."

"And die," Dallas reminded him. "Because I don't think they're taking us to their leader so they can throw us a welcome party."

"We don't know that," North said.

"It doesn't take a genius to figure it out," Holli snapped. "They killed Jeannie and C-Rod in cold blood, for Christ sakes."

"Yet they haven't killed us," North said. "Have you stopped to wonder why?"

"I have," Sherm said. "You don't want to hear what I think."

There was no point talking to North. The guy was out to lunch, not that she could blame him. Dallas turned away from the doctor. Holli was about to call out to Nichols and try to wake him from his fugue when one of the glowing birds came spiraling toward her. She put up her arms to protect her face. The bird grazed her forearm before zipping away, leaving a faint trail of luminescence in its wake.

More than half of the birds that had been circling above them, providing light, followed it. The light dimmed considerably.

Holli had never been a fan of the dark. In fact, she'd been hoping a winter wrapped in the total darkness of the South Pole would have cured her of it. The timpani march of her heart was proof it hadn't worked.

The long passageway took a near ninety-degree turn. She couldn't see what was coming up next, but there was far more light around the bend.

"End of the line," she muttered to herself, feeling the declining slope begin to even out.

The giant twisted his massive head toward her, his mouth a deep-set slash set in his pale, pale face. She'd never met a person or animal where she couldn't read some kind of emotion.

No, she was wrong. Reptiles. She'd had a boyfriend who kept all kinds of snakes and lizards. His living room walls had been filled with tanks containing his disturbing collection of pets. The face of a reptile was as cold and devoid of expression as the South Pole plains. So was her boyfriend. Was his name Zach? The relationship hadn't lasted long. She often wondered if Zach had been attracted to reptiles because he felt a kinship with them, or if being surrounded by the snakes and lizards had somehow altered his personality, wiped it clean of any nuance.

When the giant turned her body so she could see what lay ahead, she couldn't stop herself from crying out.

The tunnel opened into a cavern so large it made her dizzy just trying to look up or down. The bat men and their beasts gathered on a massive ledge, overlooking the bizarre underground world.

Holli heard the flutter of wings as the glowing birds joined the millions of their flock that swooped about the cavern, giving it the full light of day.

What lay below was a circular expanse, at least it appeared to be because the further arcs of the circle were too far away to see. There were no structures, so to speak. Nor was there any kind of plant life. The ground itself was yellowed with age, occasional blocks of dirty ice jutting from the frozen floor. In the distance was a long, wide lake, its crimson waters rippling from a breeze Holli couldn't feel from up high on the ledge. The shore of the lake was jammed with bodies too far away and indistinct to tell if they were man or animal, organic or inorganic.

But that wasn't what had socked the breath from her lungs.

For everywhere she looked, there were people milling about. Hairless, pale as death people with massive black eyes.

What chilled her more than anything she'd seen this night was the way all of those people stopped moving the second Holli's entourage stepped onto the ledge. As one, what could be millions of empty faces tilted up to view the incoming strangers.

Holli thought she was going to be sick. It was impossible to keep her stomach from opening up onto the back of the beast the giant rode upon.

"Wow," North said, his voice sounding as if he were looking upon one of the world's great mysteries. Which, in fact he was, but it irked Holli that he'd become so enraptured by it. This was not something to marvel at. She was aware of the doctor's death wish. He'd confided it to her one night after they'd both had a little too much to drink. At the time, his confession had broken her heart.

He was certainly going to get what he came down here for.

"Well fuck me sideways," Dallas gasped.

"Dear God, no," Sherm cried out. He was being pulled off the back of the ragged animal, a throng of men grasping his arms and legs, carrying him to the edge of the cliff.

"Let him go!" Holli screamed.

Dallas suddenly jumped from his position, managing to land away from the bat men that had kept him in check. He ran to Sherm, shouldering past the other men that had become living statues, their gaze locked on Sherm struggling not to be thrown to his death.

He got close enough to grab the back of the head of a man that had a tight grip on Sherm's ankle. Dallas twisted the bat-man's head until his neck snapped. The bat-man relinquished his hold, falling to the floor in a loose heap.

"Kill them!" Holli encouraged him. She felt the giant's hold on her loosen enough for her hands to reach the zipper of her Big Red. With a savage tug, she pulled the zipper down, the jacket opening like a split abdomen, spilling Holli out as if she were a mass of innards. She hit the ground hard, pain rocketing up her knees and hands. One of her wrists made a popping sound that, if she weren't numb with shock, would have kept her on the ground cradling her arm.

Instead, she ran to join Dallas.

Dallas went for another, putting his knee in the man's back and cupping his hand under his chin, bending him back until his spine made a gut-churning snap. He was about to go for a third when an ear-piercing roar brought everything to an eerie standstill.

CHAPTER TWENTY-EIGHT

Sherm peered down at the mass of waiting hominids (because he couldn't rightly say they were fully human) and his mind began to snap like dried stalks of wheat.

Between him and the waiting throng was what looked like an endless expanse of empty, frigid air.

He opened his mouth to scream, though no sound escaped. His sheer terror had paralyzed his vocal cords.

They're going to throw me off the cliff!

For a very good reason, this terrified him far more than anything he had faced so far.

A burst of adrenaline hit his body so hard, it was like touching a live wire. He went into full panic mode, every muscle flexing and fighting for release. His back arched until it felt as if his spine would snap. He tried to pull his arms and legs out of the iron grip of the men.

One leg slipped free. He was unaware that Dallas had killed the bat-man that had been holding it. Sherm continued to vibrate, fighting like a mad dog to be let down.

But the men were stronger than his burning desire not to be sent aloft.

Tears streamed from his eyes. His mouth became dry as sand.

"Please, God, no!" he pleaded, his voice a garbled whisper.

He'd fallen once before.

His father had thought the cruise to Alaska, while beautiful, hadn't given them a full appreciation of the splendor of the unspoiled country. On their stop in Skagway, he'd chartered a bush pilot to fly them above the remote terrain so they could take in the sights no tour stop would see. Sherm, his mother, father and sister boarded the small plane buzzing with excitement. They were going to take an hour tour, and then go to the special kid's show and dinner back on the ship. Sherm had also been promised he could buy any five comic books he wanted from a general store they'd passed on the way to the plane. For a six year old, it promised to be one of the most exciting days of his life.

The pilot was an Air Force vet who had flown in Vietnam, then for a commercial airline for ten years before deciding he preferred the wilds of Alaska to the suburbs of Pittsburgh. He'd told them it would be a trip they'd never forget.

Sherm certainly hadn't.

The blast of wind sheer came early into the flight. One second Sherm was looking at the unbroken vista of trees, his imagination populating the woods with all sorts of creatures, real and mythical. The next, they were spiraling down, the nose of the plane dipping until Sherm's stomach was in the back of his throat.

They fell. His parents and sister screamed. The pilot silently fought to regain control.

He didn't succeed.

Only Sherm survived. He'd been dubbed the miracle boy by all the newspapers and media outlets.

Nightmares of falling, his body greedily embraced by gravity, had plagued him for years. Flying was only possible by taking heavy doses of Xanax. His career took him all over the world. It was either take enough medication to knock out a rhino, or leave his passion behind. The choice, though simple, made every assignment complicated. He remembered nothing of his flight to Antarctica, and that was the way he liked it.

Because he never wanted to fall again.

Something cried out that chilled him to the bone. The inexorable push to shove him over the ledge ceased. Sherm was sure he could feel his ribcage cracking from trying to keep his heart from bursting free.

A shadow passed overhead.

"What?"

An albino stingray the size of a twin engine plane soared over the ledge. Its long, pointed tail swished back and forth like a whip. Sherm saw its long, toothless slit for a mouth on its pale underside. It flew effortlessly, though it had no viable means of propulsion outside of the water.

When the lipless mouth opened, out came that high, keening wail again.

The men around him dropped to their knees, their heads bowed.

Sherm was suddenly free.

Dallas helped him to his feet. The men looked up into the alabaster belly of the flying stingray.

"Is that what I think it is?" Dallas said.

"It is…but it can't be."

The giant stingray rode the unseen current, circling above in long, lazy loops. There was pressure on Sherm's shoulder. He turned to see Holli, her head tilted upward, mouth wide open.

Total silence filled the cavern until Sherm thought his ears would pop.

As the stingray swept over them, Sherm saw something played out on its underside.

"No."

Images flickered as if projected on a movie screen. They came and went in the blink of an eye. "Did you see that?" he asked Dallas and Holli.

"See what?" Holli said.

Sherm felt numb, weightless. He looked to Dallas. "You?"

The maintenance manager tugged at his beard. "What did you see?"

Sherm was about to try to put it into words when the entirety of the stingray's body came alive, the light so intense it was blinding.

"Gahhh!" Sherm shielded his watering eyes, but he couldn't look away.

"What is it? Are you ok?" Holli asked, latching onto his arm.

His mind reeled. The movie played on, the sharpness of the images like chef's knives, slicing into him.

"There!" he shouted, trembling. "You *have* to see it!"

Holli looked at Sherm, then the stingray, going back and forth several times. "Yes, we all see it. I don't think it can really be a stingray, but there it is."

He jabbed his finger in the air. "Nononono! That! Why is it doing this to me?"

Dallas stared at him, his face etched with concern.

They didn't see. Sherm didn't know how it was possible, but the awful display could only be seen by him.

Sherm watched in horror as the tiny bush plane continued its descent. The image zoomed to the interior of the plane. He saw his mother grab his father, both of them screaming, his mother's tears tracing into her hairline. His sister's eyes went as wide and pale as hard boiled eggs. Now she was screaming.

Only Sherm remained silent, his nose pressed against the window, watching the ground rush up toward them.

He watched his family fall. It was one thing to revisit it in his nightmares. This Technicolor capturing of the moment his family ceased to be was more than he could take.

The lush greenery was suddenly everywhere. The cabin exploded. Sherm's side of the plane bowed outward and his seat was sent spiraling into the trees. It wedged itself into low hanging branches where young Sherm, when he came to, would unbuckle himself and climb down the knobby tree.

This time, the nightmare was filled with the details he'd been spared. He saw the bodies of his parents and sister explode as they were crushed by the compacting plane. Blood and bone splattered the demolished interior, cutting their screams off instantly.

"Mommy! Daddy!" Sherm cried.

Holli shook him, but he couldn't look away.

He pushed her arm.

The stingray made a sharp turn, descending.

"Get down!" Dallas barked, grabbing hold of Sherm's jacket. Sherm refused to move.

The stingray soared closer and closer…falling.

Sherm's knees were locked, his eyes burning.

When the stingray swooped over their heads, its belly just inches from the top of Sherm's, it brought a powerful gust of wind that punched him in the chest.

His feet shuffled to keep his balance, until they no longer touched the ground.

Sherm rode the breeze as gently as the stingray. He heard Holli and Dallas shout after him. The edge of the cliff skidded past him and he was alone, aloft, flying.

He looked up. The stingray was climbing back to its previous height. But it left him a departing image.

His mother's head, the left side caved in, lay on its side, wedged between two seat cushions.

When he started to fall, he screamed. He screamed until something snapped in his throat. His hands clutched at the air. He begged to be saved, to not fall.

There was no one close to hear his plea.

CHAPTER TWENTY-NINE

Holli had to turn away, sobbing into her cupped hands.

Dallas wished he were smart enough to do the same. He watched Sherm fall, heard his cries until he was too far gone to see. But before that instant when the chasm between them became too great, he saw something that jolted him to his core.

It may have been a trick of the light, or just a hallucination conjured from a brain on overload. In the instant before Sherm dropped out of sight, Dallas swore he saw the man change. In that terrible flash of time, Sherm's face turned white as marble, his eyes expanding, darkening, until they were as big and black as a pair of eight balls.

It was as if he'd become *one of them*, the bat men, moments before his body joined the throng at terminal velocity.

He pulled Holli close to him, unable to look away.

Together, they shuffled around the prostrate bat men until he was close enough to look over the cliff.

All he could see was a sea of white, the men packed so tight where Sherm would have landed, there barely seemed room enough to move.

"Come on," Dallas said, hustling them away. There was nothing to see, and he didn't want one of the bat men seizing the opportunity to easily shove them both over.

Holli wiped her eyes and looked up. The stingray was gone.

"What did he see?" she asked, sniffing back tears.

"I don't know, but it sure scared the hell out of him." Dallas wasn't entirely sure of what he'd seen himself, Sherm's impossible transformation deepening his sense of dread.

He looked over at North who was still atop one of the animals. The doctor was watching the giant, who had spread his arms wide, head thrown back.

"What's he doing?" Dallas said.

"It looks like the fucker's basking in the afterglow of Sherm's death," Holli said icily.

There was a shift in the atmosphere, a slight rumbling Dallas could feel through his boots. "I don't think that's it."

The bat men closest to the cliff's edge stood and jerkily shifted away, nearly knocking Dallas and Holli down in their haste. "Oh, that's not good," Dallas said, wrapping his arms around Holli. He tried to move further back, but they smacked against the solid wall of men.

North was roughly removed from the creature and tossed in their direction. He landed hard on his hip, crying out in pain. Nichols was thrown as well, though when he hit the ground he did so silently, lying there as if he were dead. Dallas pulled away from Holli to help North up.

"You okay?"

North grimaced, massaging his hip. "I'd have broken something if not for these layers."

"Help me get Nichols to his feet."

They straddled Nichols and lifted. Nichols managed to stand on his own two feet, though his eyes were glassy, staring into the expanse. Dallas snapped his fingers inches from Nichols' face.

"Come on, Nichols. You gotta snap out of it."

The man didn't even blink.

"You think Jeannie would want you to be like this? We're going to *need* you, not *carry* you."

There was a faint glimmer of recognition, a slight twitching of his mouth, but that was all.

That suddenly became the least of Dallas' worries.

The rumbling grew louder, escalating until it was the thunder of wild horses approaching. They looked around for the source of the cacophony.

"What now?" Holli said.

Dallas ran to the edge of the cliff, got on his hands and knees and looked down.

He scrambled away, falling on his ass in desperation to get away.

"Run!" he shouted.

He hooked an arm around Nichols and took off, only to be pushed back as if he were made of paper by the iron throng of bat men. Holli tugged at him. "What is it? What is it?"

The first of the new and horrid creatures hooked its gargantuan claws into the icy ledge and pulled itself up.

Even North screamed this time.

It was essentially a bat, pale as death and as big as a van. Its fangs were as long as a man's forearm. The giant bat's pale pink eyes locked onto them and it shrieked. It got its legs under it – legs that were as thick and powerful as a Clydesdale's. It was joined by more and more bats, all as identical as the first.

Dallas shoved Holli behind him.

"You still fascinated?" he said to North.

The doctor's mouth opened and closed, opened and closed, not a single word escaping.

When Dallas turned around to see if there was any chance the men had broken up, offering a means of escape, he saw that they all had their arms thrust outward, heads back, just like their giant leader.

The bats had formidable talons on the ends of their leathery wings. With each step they took, they slammed the talons into the ground, piercing it as if it were hot butter.

They screeched as one and the sound nearly burst Dallas' eardrums. He slapped his hands over his ears, but it was too little, too late. The sonic assault made his vision waver. He was so dizzy, he had a hard time staying on his feet. What was up seemed down.

He slammed his eyes shut, hoping the darkness would restore his equilibrium.

When he opened them several moments later, the enormous bats were standing over them.

"Oh shit, no," Holli panted.

The stench of burnt matches rolled off the winged beasts. Dallas balled his hands into fists in what he knew would be a futile attempt to defend himself, to defend them all.

One of the bats dipped its furry head toward him, a thick rope of saliva dripping from its maw. It opened its mouth, showing Dallas the rows of teeth it had in store for him. Dallas decided at that moment he would die fighting before getting sucked into its mouth and shredded alive.

He was about to punch it in its snout when the rippling of its belly stopped him cold. The fur wriggled and moved as if something were trying to burrow free.

CHAPTER THIRTY

North's skin wanted to crawl off his bones and fly far away from here. He'd always hated bats. Growing up in rural Massachusetts, bats often got into the house, causing an instant ruckus, eliciting terrified peals from his sisters. He'd once had a bat fly directly into his face, knocking him over a chair. From that moment on, North would run into the nearest closet when a bat infiltrated their home. When night fell and the air was ripe with them, he would stay indoors, even when his friends were still outside and calling him a chicken.

Those were harmless fruit bats.

These pale, beastly specimens were too horrifying to behold. North wanted to close his eyes and wish them away.

"I don't fucking believe it," Dallas said.

Neither did North.

As if being a giant, ivory bat wasn't enough, North stared in stark horror as massive arms, the arms of a human bodybuilder, burst from the bats' abdomens.

A pair of arms grabbed North, pulling him into the bat's sulfur-smelling body. He opened his mouth to scream and found it filled with bristly fibers. He jerked his head sideways, the coarse hair scratching his face like nails. His heartbeat was a manic metronome pounding in his ears. He saw Dallas, Holli and Nichols embraced by the bats and their impossible fresh set of arms.

And then they were climbing up into the air. North's stomach dropped, bile spewing from his open mouth.

He heard screaming.

It was his own.

His body went stiff as a board. He wanted nothing more than to extricate himself from the bat's clutches, but he also knew that if he managed to struggle free, he'd only fall to his death. Like Sherm.

North squeezed his eyes shut, but not tight enough to stop the flow of tears. His atavistic repulsion of bats fought against his will to survive, a will he thought he'd lost. He knew from the moment the base had been destroyed that there was no coming back, but he didn't want to die before he'd seen all he could see.

And now he didn't want to see any more. Yet he wanted to live.

No, that wasn't exactly right.

He still deeply missed his wife. Everyday without her had been empty and lonely, even when he was surrounded by friends and family. But there was comfort in knowing that they would meet again in the hereafter. Many nights when he went to bed, he prayed he'd never wake up, at least in this world.

North had wanted to die all these years. He just didn't want to die like this, his last moments plagued by fear and pain.

His mind reeled as the bat twisted in the air. He felt he was seconds from passing out, which would be a mercy. North willed the bat to do more aerial acrobatics, to put him out of his misery.

The bat responded by leveling out, flying straight and steady. It was as if it could read his mind, taking delight in defying his wishes.

No!

North let his panic run rampant. His heart rate escalated. His breath came in short, pained gasps. He was starting to hyperventilate. This was good. Sooner or later, he would grow fuzzy, his brain shutting down from the lack of oxygen. He thought he heard Holli say something, but her voice sounded so, so far away.

The tang of blood filled his mouth. He realized the bat's fur had cut deep furrows in his face. The wounds seeped into his mouth as he gulped for air.

Please, please, please, pass the fuck out!

Was it possible to do so while you were still able to desperately want it to happen? He'd never encountered a patient who'd told him such a thing.

His stomach flipped again as the bat changed elevation.

He dared to open his eyes.

They were descending.

There was no sign of the other giant bats.

The bat sailed over the pale, bald heads of the countless men crammed along the cavern floor. They reached up, their fingers brushing against North's rigid body as the bat lowered itself even further. North felt his bowels let loose the same moment he unleashed a terrific wail.

And then it all stopped.

The powerful arms let North go. He dropped several feet onto the icy ground. The men had pulled away, making a clearing for him.

The ground shook steadily. It was not the quaking of aftershocks. It was the booming, steady approach of something humongous.

On his hands and knees, weeping, North refused to open his eyes. He didn't want to see what was coming. He didn't want to see anything anymore. Only his wife.

"Rose, please, take me with you! Please, Rose, come save me!"

"Stand!"

The command cut North's pleas as quickly as the sharp snap of a faucet.

"Stand!"

The deep, bass tone of the voice shook North's bones, rattling his already erratic heart.

It was a voice that was not to be ignored.

North pushed himself up, still keeping his eyes closed, conjuring images of his Rose, hoping if he thought of her and only her, she could reach out between the veil and pull him toward the warmth, safety and comfort of her bosom.

"Look!"

North shook his head.

Hands grabbed him painfully, making him cry out.

Several of the bat men had lunged to grasp his arms, their fingers pinching through muscle until their tips hit bone. His nerves were on fire. His eyes popped open, eyes bulging from the rush of pain.

He saw the man behind the voice.

This monster made the giant that had led their capture look like a Lilliputian.

This new, astounding giant stood no less than thirty feet tall. His muscles rippled as he walked, hands flexing as if he were preparing to crush North to death. He was paler than death, with a slash for a mouth that went so far back, the corners disappeared behind the back of his head. His black eyes were as big as a man curled in the fetal position. North saw sparks of red in those eyes, dancing, bloody fireflies swirling in their centers.

"See," the giant said.

He opened his hands, thrusting his palms outward until they were a mere foot from his face.

In one palm, North saw Rose, poor, emaciated Rose, lying on her deathbed in the hospice. Her body had been reduced to sticks, her teeth rotted out, mouth open wide. And there he was beside her, holding her hand, telling her it was all right to let go, silent tears running down his cheeks. Her chest heaved once, twice, and fell, never to rise again. What little was left of her sagged deeper into the bed. North wept, whispering, "Wait for me in Heaven, honey. Wait for me."

The hand closed. North felt what little strength and will he had left, break.

"Now, look," the giant commanded.

In the other palm, there was nothing but endless black.

North stared into the pitch, searching for something.

"Look!" the giant roared.

"I…I am."

His eyes darted to every corner of the open hand. It was like looking into the dark reaches of the South Pole during the endless night, except he couldn't look up and see stars or the moon.

"I don't…I don't see anything," he whimpered.

The hand closed and the giant grinned, the crescent of its smile stretching to the top of its head.

"Yesssss. Nothing."

North stared at the beast of a man, dumfounded.

And he suddenly understood.

"No!" North blurted.

The giant began to chuckle. It escalated to maniacal laughing.

North sagged, only the piercing hands of the men keeping him upright.

It couldn't be true. Rose was not gone forever. There had to be more than that.

His belief was shattered by the giant's revelation.

She would not be waiting for him. She was truly and forever gone. There had never been any hope.

North wept, his cries drowned out by the giant's rumbling laughter. He was let go, falling to his knees.

A powerful rush of air knocked him backward.

He looked up, wiping his eyes with the back of his hand so he could see.

The giant bat had returned.

Looking up, past the bat's vermin-like face, he spotted the others. Holli, Dallas and Nichols were still up there, circling.

Soon enough, they would be brought down. And they would know.

The bat's arms scooped him up.

He was gently, almost tenderly, lifted towards its mouth. North snapped his head down. He did not want to stare into the beast's waiting, hungry mouth. With a great shudder, he felt something let go in the core of his body. His skin felt as if it were on fire. When he looked down, his hands were not his own. They had been replaced by chalk white, muscular hands. He didn't have time to puzzle what had happened.

The bat's mouth closed upon his neck, but its teeth did not penetrate his flesh. Encased in the darkness of its mouth, North went stark raving mad, flailing and screaming until his heart, in its final act of kindness, burst.

CHAPTER THIRTY-ONE

Dallas had never felt so helpless…and repulsed. It was bad enough to watch those massive *human* arms sprout from the trunk of a bat big enough to carry a semi off into the darkness. It was another to have them locked around his body, their vice-like grip impossible to break out of.

It was also no bed of roses having his face smashed against the vile underside of the bat. Its hair felt like tiny needles. He was sure he looked like he'd had his face dragged behind a car over a gravel driveway.

He saw Holli to his right. She had gone silent, flown too far away from him to see her face. Nichols was 'strapped' to the bat to her right.

North was nowhere to be seen.

Dallas had heard the doc's cries when those arms got ahold of him. Whatever fascination he'd had with their predicament died at that moment. He hoped to hell North was alright. The man may have gone a little bat shit – no pun intended – over the crazy life forms they'd been encountering, but that was just shock.

The bat went into a sudden nosedive. Dallas felt everything he'd ever eaten tumble up into his throat. The arms squeezed tighter, making it hard to breathe. Black spots flickered at his vision's edge.

It stopped so suddenly, Dallas felt his organs shift while the framework of his body remained locked. His brain shifted in his skull, sparking an explosion of stars. He didn't even sense the arms letting him go, nor did he have the senses to put his arms out to break his fall. The side of his face hit the floor, breaking off several molars, bounced up and slammed down again. He heard the wreckage of bone and teeth in his head as if it were in surround sound.

Groaning, spitting out thick wads of blood and teeth, Dallas tried to get his arms to work, to will his legs to move.

The ice cold floor beckoned him to stay. The cold felt good on his damaged face.

Maybe I'll just rest here a minute, he thought. It hurt to even think about lifting his head.

He looked around, but could only see white. He blew out a sharp breath, scattering light flakes of snow. It took the phrase *being snow blind* to a whole new level.

Dallas had been in his fair share of physical scrapes, but he'd never had his bell rung. Until now. As much as the rational part of him shouted to get up, the majority ruling part of his brain and his entire body refused to listen.

Even Holli's screams couldn't rouse him.

Dallas closed his eyes with the intention of going to see what was happening to Holli. Instead, he slipped into a dreamless slumber.

When the bat's man-arms dropped Holli, she managed to pull her legs up and hit the ground on her heels. She slid along the slick ground for several feet before hammering her tailbone. A hot lance of pain went from the base of her spine through the top of her head. It punched the breath out of her. She fell onto her back, spinning as momentum carried her past Dallas who lay face down, his arms at his side as if he'd died somewhere in the air. Nichols was nowhere to be found. She had no idea where North could be.

The moment she stopped, both hands went to her rump. She howled in agony. For a second, she thought her cries had scared the bats away, but she quickly realized the winged monsters had delivered them to whatever fresh nightmare this was going to be and left them to the next level of torture.

It hurt to stand, much less walk, so bad she worried she'd broken something. Holli limped her way to Dallas, calling his name, hoping for some kind of response. If he was dead and she was left here on her own, she was sure she'd lose the tiny shreds of sanity she had left.

"Come on, boss," she said, standing over him and wondering how she was going to manage to crouch down to check him out. If he wasn't breathing, she worried she wouldn't remember a thing from the CPR class she'd taken ten years ago. A thin puddle of blood spilled out of his mouth. "If you die on me, so help me, I'll kill you."

A wave of nausea hit her as she canted to one knee. Holli swept the snow away from his face. How could snow get down here? Maybe, she thought, it was tiny flakes of ice. Unless this place was large enough to have its own atmosphere. At this point, she'd believe anything was possible.

She touched Dallas' cheek. It was cold, but his closed eye flinched. She exhaled a great plume of fog with relief. "Time to get up."

She saw the shattered teeth and his split lips as she turned his head to the side. His groan, followed by, "What in the hell are you doing?" were the best sounds she'd ever heard.

"You took a nap," she said. "We don't have time for naps."

Looking around, she didn't see anything or anyone nearby. Where had the bats dumped them?

Dallas coughed, spitting up a bloody wad of phlegm. "Hols, you were either hiding a pair of twin sisters, or I'm seeing triple." He clutched the sides of his head. His eyes were dancing in their sockets.

"I think you have a concussion," she said. "I'll take that over a broken ass bone." When she shifted to stand, the pain practically paralyzed her.

"It's because you're too skinny," he said, the half-smile on his ruined face a sight to scare children. "If you had more padding, you'd be fine."

Together, they helped each other to their feet, one as crippled as the other. "You know a local all-you-can-eat buffet and I'll keep filling my plate until I pop. I want to get out of here so bad, I'd even settle for a Golden Corral."

Keeping one eye closed, Dallas said, "So, where do we go from here?"

A gust of wind, warbling like a lone owl, whipped overhead. There was nothing but the vast emptiness of pale, misty landscape as far as they could see. If Holli hadn't known better, she would think they had been deposited right back at Freedom Base, minus the wreckage.

"Whichever way points home," Holli said.

Dallas put his hand on her shoulder. "I don't think there is a way."

Her molars worried at the inside of her cheek until her tongue tasted old pennies. "Yeah, I don't think so either."

"We could always just rest a while and wait to see what they have in store for us next."

Holli shook her head. "I can't. It's not in me to just sit around and wait for some disaster to happen."

Wheezing, Dallas put a hand on his ribs. "If you were old like me and broken – think I might have fractured a rib or three – waiting has a whole new appeal."

"What we need to do is find North and Nichols."

A shiver rushed through her, making all the sore parts hurt even more. It was cold as hell in this underworld, though not so cold that they were in imminent danger of freezing to death. But freeze to death they would if they decided to just lie down and take a little siesta.

Though dying in their sleep seemed the most appealing outcome to their situation.

"You see which direction they went?" Dallas asked.

"Nope. In fact, I didn't see North at all. Nichols was beside me, at least until that freaking bat made its way down here."

Dallas pointed over her shoulder. "Let's go that way, then. Seems as good a place to start as any."

Actually, it looked like every other place to start. Without a compass or anything to serve as a reference point, they could easily walk in circles until their bodies gave out.

As they limped along, Holli said, "You still seeing triple?"

"Only if I keep both eyes open."

They walked and walked, each calling out for Nichols and North from time to time. There was no way to tell how long they kept at it or which direction they were going. There was no sun in the sky to guide them. Just those illuminated birds, constantly swarming far above. Their light played against the growing fog, creating strange and wondrous light displays in the ground mist.

Holli was hurt and hungry and running out of gas. If this was how it ended, taking the big cold sleep when her legs could no longer take another step, she would consider it a blessing. But until then, she was going to give every ounce of strength she had to finding those two men. Everyone may die alone, but it was always more comforting to do it beside another.

Dallas' breathing was sounding worse and worse. He was spitting up less blood as the wounds in his mouth dried up, but she worried one of his ribs had pierced a lung.

"North! Nichols! Can you here me?" she shouted for the umpteenth time.

The wind answered her.

Dallas faltered. He latched onto her arm and as he fell, he dragged her down with him. Holli yelped as she angled her body so her thigh took the brunt of the fall.

"I'm done, Hols," Dallas panted. "Stick in the fork. Maybe this is what those things wanted. Just leave us to die."

"I can't believe that," she said. "I mean, why drag us down here in the first place? They could have killed us as easily as they did Jeannie and C-Rod at the base. It just doesn't make sense."

He waved at the air between them. "There's no point in trying to make sense out of any of this. We got in their way, they took an interest in us for a spell, and now we're like all those shiny toys the week after Christmas."

"Especially the broken toys."

"Especially them.

"Look, you can keep looking for them, but me, I can't get up. My head feels like it's going to split in two and I can't see straight. Shit, I'm having a hard time remembering my address and my girlfriend's name. If you find North or Nichols, come back and get me."

Holli knew if she found them, she'd never be able to locate Dallas.

She was about to tell him to quit feeling sorry for himself and get off his ass when she spotted a snow-covered mound ahead of them.

"Do you believe in miracles?" she said as she painfully got back on her feet.

"Only if the day comes where I'm back in my lounge chair with a beer in one hand and cigar in the other."

Holli patted his chest and did the closest approximation to a run as she could muster.

CHAPTER THIRTY-TWO

Ignoring the flaring pain in her back and hips, Holli slid to her knees. The Big Red jacket was covered in a fine layer of white flakes, the wearer's back turned to her. She didn't know whether it was North or Nichols, and she hesitated turning them over in case they had internal injuries. Then she realized even if they did, there was no way to call 911 here in the frozen bowels of the Earth.

She grabbed the sleeve of the Big Red and pulled.

"Nichols."

His eyes were wide open. She knew in an instant he hadn't survived the fall.

Or maybe his heart simply broke, she thought. *Seeing Jeannie killed like that was the same as driving a dagger through his chest.*

She'd never encountered a couple so in love before. Coming from her fucked up home, Holli had no grounding for what a healthy relationship could look like. Even her own short-lived romances were always tainted by her mistrust and anger.

Holli tried to sit, but the rockets of pain drove her onto her side where she fell into the cold grip of uncontrollable sobbing. She wept for Nichols and Jeannie, C-Rod and Sherm. She wept out of pain and fear and a well of hopelessness deeper than the inexorable end of a black hole.

Through the shimmer of tears, she searched for Dallas, who had only been thirty or so feet from Nichols. She couldn't find him. She had a feeling no matter how far or hard she looked, this place wouldn't allow them to reunite. It had gotten what it wanted.

In the end, she sobbed over her total isolation.

Every time her chest hitched, her thinking went fuzzy as the pain in her lower back escalated. Still, she let the tears come, encouraged herself to cry and cry until her brain shut it all down.

She should stop, try to find North.

He was probably dead, too.

Dallas would be soon, if he wasn't already, wherever he was.

Holli wiped her face, her hand having grown so numb, she couldn't feel it at all anymore. Her tears melted the snow.

She lay there, letting her emotions run free, unaware of the passage of time or the steady drop in temperature. Her toes burned with encroaching frostbite.

It was a long while before she was all cried out. She'd never lost consciousness, coming close many times.

"Fuck it," she sniffled.

She used the inside of her Big Red to dry her face. Her cheeks hurt like hell as the rough fabric brushed against them. She imagined her face was as bright as a freshly picked apple – raw and close to bleeding.

"I want to go home. I want to go home. I want to go home."

In the middle of her Dorothy-like chanting, she saw them.

The bat men were coming. Hundreds of them. No, thousands. She placed her palm against the frozen ground and felt the beat of their syncopated march.

They'd broken her, and now they were coming to devour the pieces.

Dallas' eyes snapped open when he felt the tremors.

He looked around for Holli, hoping that North and Nichols were in tow.

It wasn't them.

What he did see were those bald bat men heading his way.

There was no fight left in him.

Dallas lay on his back, hands folded across his chest, and waited. If they expected a struggle, they would be sorely disappointed. He'd been hoping he'd be a rock-hard popsicle by the time they found him, all his cares and worries gone into the ether. He should have known he wouldn't be so lucky.

One last indignity before I get to call it quits.

"Come on!" he heard Holli scream.

She sounded close. When she'd walked away to look for their missing comrades, it was as if the ground mist had conspired to swallow her up. She went no more than five feet from him before disappearing into the swirling mist. He'd assumed they'd never see each other again.

"Hols!" he shouted.

"Dallas?"

"Keep talking. I'll come to you." He winced as he ordered his body to get up. "You find them?"

"It's Nichols," she replied. "He's dead."

He refrained from saying, *lucky bastard.*

Eyeballing the men – they were a hundred yards out and steadily making their way – Dallas said, "Keep talking so I can follow your voice."

As if in answer to his plea, the fog thickened, rising up from around his knees to eye level. Dammit! This cursed place did everything in its power to make your life miserable.

"You know what I could go for right now?" Holli said.

"What?" Talking loud enough for her to hear him hurt like blue, black and white blazes.

"A nuclear bomb. I'd drop it right on their asses and fry them where they stand."

"I'd go for that."

He stutter-stepped, homing in on her voice.

"I don't care if I get turned to crispy bacon in the process. I just ask that I get a few seconds to watch these fuckers melt," Holli said.

"It would be nice to incinerate this whole damn place," he said. "Not sure we want what's here getting out."

All along, that had been a growing concern. If the earthquake had set these things loose, how much destruction would and could they wreak? Would the other Antarctic bases be next? There was nothing in the bitter tundra that could stop them. Once they'd conquered Antarctica, would they advance north? Could they withstand the warmth of, say, Australia and beyond? He hoped not. He hoped they'd fry like ants under the Aussie sun.

"But before all that," Holli continued. "I'd kill for an In-N-Out burger. Actually, three In-N-Out burgers. With two large orders of fries, a vanilla milkshake and two Cokes."

"In-N-Out burger, huh? Never had one."

"Then you haven't lived."

And I won't much longer, Dallas thought.

"Sorry," Holli said.

"No need to be, Hols."

And then he saw her. She was lying next to Nichols, his face turned to the false sky, eyes open and most likely a pair of frozen cue balls with pupils. He saw the bat men were now fifty yards off.

Holli somehow managed to leap to her feet and wrap her arms around him. "Don't let me go," she said, her teeth chattering.

He slipped his arm around her waist, one hand on the back of her head, pulling her to his chest. "I won't. I promise."

The mist blew away even though there was no breeze. Dallas looked over Holli's shoulder at poor Nichols.

He went rigid.

"Hols."

"What?" she said into his chest.

"Look."

She pulled herself away to see what he was looking at. Her eyes fell on Nichols.

And the wisps of vapor coming from his mouth.

Dallas croaked, "He's alive."

CHAPTER THIRTY-THREE

"Oh my God!"

Holli broke away from Dallas' assuring embrace. She put her hands on Nichols' shoulders and gently rocked him. "Nichols. Can you hear me?"

His eyes didn't blink, didn't so much as flick in her direction. They stared blankly up at the circling birds.

"He's still gone," she said to Dallas.

"Maybe it's better that way."

The bat men were almost upon them.

Holli whipped around, her heart racing. She'd been resigned to whatever terrifying thing they were going to do to them, defiantly so, but that resolve had dissipated like the fog in their menacing presence.

Dallas reached down and grabbed her hand, helping her to her feet.

The giant man wasn't among them. These were just the anonymous minions. Not that that brought any sense of comfort.

The men stopped several feet from them, their big, black eyes staring, mouths shut so tight, it almost looked as if they had no mouths at all.

Holli and Dallas stood their ground. She could feel Dallas' body shaking under his layers.

The ground shook.

Boom.

Boom.

BOOM!

Holli turned around. They'd been so focused on the army of bat men, they hadn't noticed the enormous man who seemed to have risen up from the ground itself.

Her blood ran colder than the darkest winter night in the South Pole.

The man before them was similar to the other bat men in that he was white as chalk with nary a hair on his body and eyes so large, entire armies could fall to their death in them. He stood at least fifty feet tall. Holli's neck cracked as she tried to take in the vast behemoth.

Oh the sides of his head were massive, curved horns. An evil, horrid smile split his wide face.

On the tips of his fingers were nails the size of surfboards, the tips honed to fine, deadly points. She watched, her mouth agape, as he flicked the index finger of his right hand across the wrist of his left hand. The skin split wide open.

Except there was no blood.

What looked like balls of hail spilled from the open wound. They cascaded onto the ground. Holli looked in horror as the hail rolled, then sprouted eight sets of legs.

Spiders!

Thousands of spiders erupted from the rent in the giant's flesh.

Dallas said something that sounded like gibberish to her. What was there to possibly say before such a sight?

The spiders skittered their way.

Holli tried to scream, but her throat felt as if it had been stuffed with dry, dirty rags.

She turned to run, but they had been hemmed in by the throng of bat men.

The giant bellowed with laughter.

"They want you…Holli."

Hearing her name spoken by the behemoth man nearly stopped her heart.

Dallas tried to shield her, but she couldn't move.

Her eyes opened wider and wider as the pale spiders came.

They want you, Holli.

As they came closer, she saw they weren't just spiders.

She could see their faces.

"No!" she peeled. "Nononononononononononono!"

Her stepfather's face, the molesting piece of garbage that had ruined her childhood, infected every waking moment of her life, was plastered on each and every one of the spiders. The faces licked their lips in anticipation, just as he would do before he slipped his fingers under the waistband of her Power Rangers pajamas.

"You know you miss us," the spiders cried in his voice times ten thousand. "You know you like it."

"Stop talking!" she shouted.

"I didn't say anything," Dallas said beside her. She'd forgotten all about him. Her flesh crawled at the sight of her arachnid step-fathers.

"Just take my finger and put it where you like it," the spiders cooed, their spindly legs flittering as they came for her.

One spider, faster than the others, quicker than lightning, was instantly at her feet. Holli wasted no time stomping it to paste.

She felt it pop beneath her boot. But there was no moment of joy. There was no way she could squish them all. The demented fuck would have his way with her and worse.

Holli screamed and screamed, drowning out the predatory babble of the spiders.

Dallas didn't know what to do. Holli had completely lost her mind. She was talking to the spiders as if they were speaking to her. They were terrifying to look at, but he hadn't heard a thing from them, other than the *tick-tick-ticking* of their legs tapping on the ice.

When the giant had said her name, though, even Dallas had swooned. In a world of the impossible, how could that be?

He tried to get Holli behind him so he could take the brunt of the spider assault. She was as immovable as a marble statue.

"Come on, Hols," he said, tugging at her.

It was no use.

And it was too late.

The spiders swarmed up her legs, covering her with their alabaster bodies in seconds. Within the mass of the writhing spiders, he could still hear her scream.

The giant's laughter resumed.

"You fucking bastard," Dallas cried out. The spiders ignored him completely, piling onto Holli until she was brought to her knees.

The laughter stopped short.

The giant turned his enormous eyes to Dallas.

"Daaaalllllaaaassssss."

When the giant leaned down to peer at him, Dallas felt like a living butterfly, his wings pegged to a cork board, unable to move, unable to even turn away, forced to look his executioner in the eye.

Those eyes! They were blacker than the blackest moonless night.

And yet, there was something within them. A spark that began to grow the longer Dallas stared into them.

Within those black, bottomless pools, he saw the mangled bodies of a family – a woman, her two children and a baby clutched to her breast. They had been hiding in a dilapidated building in Fallujah. Dallas' platoon had been sent in to sweep any survivors out after the area had been carpeted with bombs from the screaming jets overhead. Intel said this had been a terrorist stronghold.

It may have been. But this particular building had housed the families of the men who had vowed to die in their insane jihad.

The smell of blood and freshly exposed organs, the roasted pig stench of burned flesh, came rushing back to him.

Just as he'd done then, Dallas turned away and vomited.

Only this time, the bodies began to move. Twisted and broken and rendered fleshless in spots, the woman and children rose from the floor, shambling towards him.

Dallas screeched. "No! Get away from me!"

He slammed his eyes shut, unable to take in the grisly scene.

The giant laughed.

Dallas covered his face.

Holli's cries had stopped.

He dared to look again, hoping the giant had shifted his gaze away.

The bodies fell from the giant's eyes, landing at Dallas' feet.

As they touched the ground, they turned white as snow. But they were no less horrible to look at. The baby cried, tiny, broken hands fumbling for his mother's exposed breast. Instead of the warm comfort of her bosom, there lay the open cavity of her ribcage.

Dallas wept.

The children, their faces split in two, one side flopping on their shoulders, reached up and grabbed his fingers.

They didn't try to hurt him. They didn't speak.

The dead family simply held him, the mother, the bottom part of her face gone, obliterated from the bomb, tenderly putting her arm around his neck, moving in closer for a kiss.

White hot agony ripped from the center of his chest to his left arm.

Dallas felt her tongue graze his lips.

His heart refused to stop, forcing him to live through the unholy reunion. He tried to push her away and saw his hands were now white.

If he had a mirror, he was sure he'd see a hairless, ivory face looking back at him, his eyes dark as tar and too big for his head.

The dead children nuzzled him as the mother's tongue slipped inside his mouth. His brain cried out for release.

CHAPTER THIRTY-FOUR

Nichols had watched everything unfold, yet he was unable to lift a finger to stop it. Or even to lend a moment of comfort.

Because he knew.

There was no comfort to be given here. There was no saving grace. No last minute means of escape.

Everyone was dead.

And then they were not.

His eyes rolled to the side, just in time to see Holli emerge from the spiders. Only she wasn't Holli anymore.

Rising from the now dead mass of spiders was one of the bat men. He – Holli – blinked once, looked down at her new body, and was drawn into the mass of waiting men, disappearing in plain sight.

Dallas had changed as well.

The strange beings that had surrounded him pulled away, turning to fine, white dust.

The pale man that Dallas had become sloughed off the clothes and trappings of humanity. He too was absorbed into the multitude of identical bat men.

Nichols wanted so much to scream, but nothing in his body was working. When he watched Jeannie savagely ripped to shreds, the bridge between his mind and body collapsed. Outwardly, he knew he looked like a brainless vegetable. If they only knew how his brain continued to function, unable to stop replaying Jeannie's murder over and over again.

When the giant finally looked down on him, Nichols could only stare back.

I know what you are, he thought.

He knew there was no need to give it voice. The giant could hear him loud and clear.

The giant's lips curled back. His ram's horns unfurled, slithering atop his head like snakes seeking warmth.

There's nothing more you can do to me, Nichols thought. *Nothing*.

The giant pulled back, concern pinching his awful face.

Nichols' lips trembled. His jaw became unlocked. His throat clicked as his tongue pulled painfully from the roof of his mouth.

The words sounded like they came from a different man, a man older than time and wounded by the passage of eons. "You lose…*Satan*," Nichols muttered.

The giant sneered.

"I'm not af…afraid of you. Your demons…they showed me…showed me Hell. Conjure whatever creatures…your dead heart desires. I…I don't care anymore."

The giant roared and the bat men dropped to their hands and knees, bowing their heads.

Nichols smiled.

All the scholars and prophets and evangelists and old church ladies had it wrong. Hell wasn't a pit of fire and brimstone existing solely in the void between life and death. It was here. It had always been here, right under their feet. You didn't need to die to get here. But you would die once you gazed upon it.

Maybe, Nichols thought, there were other places like this around the world, underground portals to what ancient man had termed Hell for want of a better way to describe it.

Hell was as cold and wasted as a corpse's heart.

Hell was a living, breathing place, not a soul's destination.

Nichols pushed himself into a sitting position and spat at the giant Satan, or whatever it was supposed to be. For all he knew, there was another twice as large, looming somewhere in this frozen Hell.

The giant slammed a fist into the ground next to Nichols. He lifted off the stone and ice for a moment, the exhilaration of knowing bringing animation back to his numb body.

Now it was time for Nichols to laugh.

Satan was powerless against his knowledge. Powerless to conjure anything that was worse than seeing his wife murdered before his very eyes.

Nor did Nichols fear death. In fact, he embraced it just as he had Jeannie.

The giant gnashed his teeth and roared with the bass and power of a multitude of lions.

All the while, Nichols laughed.

"You can't scare a man who's already dead," he said.

Satan reared back, arms outstretched, hands clenched into fists. His wailing made the glowing birds explode, their bodies spiraling from the sky. The giant bellowed and bleated until Hell went black and still and silent.

Something touched him.

Nichols jerked his leg back.

He couldn't see a thing.

There it was again. A gentle prodding against his calf.

Something cold. Something firm yet soft against his naked flesh.

How was this possible?

He was covered in something.

Nichols reached out with trembling hands, his fingers brushing across the fabric.

Sheets. Blankets.

His eyes adjusted to the darkness and he could suddenly make out shapes. He was in bed, the glow from the blue light of his phone charger the lone beacon in the blackness.

That pressure against his leg was Jeannie, her perpetually cold feet always seeking him out when they were under the covers.

She moaned in her sleep and he felt her forehead settle against his shoulder.

Nichols had to stifle back a sob.

"Jeannie?"

She shifted under the sheets.

His heart pounded so hard, he was sure it would wake her up. Good. He wanted her to wake up. He was desperate to see her face, to hear her voice, to hold her naked body close.

As he fumbled for the light, he paused.

What if this was a trick? What if the visions of a frozen Hell hadn't been a nightmare? Would he turn on the light only to see one of the bat men in the bed beside him?

He reached out and felt the tips of her hair, the swell of her breast.

Sagging with relief, he snapped on the light.

Jeannie, his Jeannie, instantly put her hand over her face.

"Please don't tell me it's time to get up," she said, burying her face in the pillow.

Nichols checked the clock. They had only been asleep for a couple of hours. The scent of their lovemaking was still in the room.

He leaned down and kissed her, savoring the warmth of her skin, the taste of her salt and perfume.

"No. We have time."

"Then turn the light off," she said.

He did. "I love you," Nichols said.

Jeannie was already snoring.
He put his arm around her and closed his eyes.
Soon, he was snoring too.

CHAPTER THIRTY-FIVE

"Did you hear that?"

Jeannie had thrown back the covers after jabbing him with her elbow. The room shook as if they were on a ride at an amusement park. Books flipped off the shelves.

Nichols snapped awake.

"Where are my clothes?"

Jeannie was tucking her shirt into her pants and donning a cap to cover the mass of red, bed head curls. "I don't know. Wherever you left them. Meet me in seismology when you find them."

The earthquake rumbled.

Nichols sat frozen in the bed.

He watched, helpless, as Jeannie ran out the door, shouting at him to get a move on.

He could hear Dallas and Holli yelling in the corridor.

Tears rolled down his cheeks.

The wind howled outside, battering the walls.

Within that squall, Nichols swore he heard laughter.

THE END

CHECK OUT OTHER GREAT CRYPTID NOVELS

BIGFOOT WAR
by Eric S. Brown

Now a feature film from Origin Releasing. For the first time ever, all three core books of the Bigfoot War series have been collected into a single tome of Sasquatch Apocalypse horror. Remastered and reedited this book chronicles the original war between man and beast from the initial battles in Babblecreek through the apocalypse to the wastelands of a dark future world where Sasquatch reigns supreme and mankind struggles to survive. If you think you've experienced Bigfoot Horror before, think again. Bigfoot War sets the bar for the genre and will leave you praying that you never have to go into the woods again.

CRYPTID ZOO
by Gerry Griffiths

As a child, rare and unusual animals, especially cryptid creatures, always fascinated Carter Wilde.

Now that he's an eccentric billionaire and runs the largest conglomerate of high-tech companies all over the world, he can finally achieve his wildest dream of building the most incredible theme park ever conceived on the planet...CRYPTID ZOO.

Even though there have been apparent problems with the project, Wilde still decides to send some of his marketing employees and their families on a forced vacation to assess the theme park in preparation for Opening Day.

Nick Wells and his family are some of those chosen and are about to embark on what will become the most terror-filled weekend of their lives—praying they survive.

STEP RIGHT UP AND GET YOUR FREE PASS...

TO CRYPTID ZOO

CHECK OUT OTHER GREAT CRYPTID NOVELS

SWAMP MONSTER MASSACRE
by Hunter Shea

The swamp belongs to them. Humans are only prey. Deep in the overgrown swamps of Florida, where humans rarely dare to enter, lives a race of creatures long thought to be only the stuff of legend. They walk upright but are stronger, taller and more brutal than any man. And when a small boat of tourists, held captive by a fleeing criminal, accidentally kills one of the swamp dwellers' young, the creatures are filled with a terrifyingly human emotion—a merciless lust for vengeance that will paint the trees red with blood.

TERROR MOUNTAIN
by Gerry Griffiths

When Marcus Pike inherits his grandfather's farm and moves his family out to the country, he has no idea there's an unholy terror running rampant about the mountainous farming community. Sheriff Avery Anderson has seen the heinous carnage and the mutilated bodies. He's also seen the giant footprints left in the snow—Bigfoot tracks. Meanwhile, Cole Wagner, and his wife, Kate, are prospecting their gold claim farther up the valley, unaware of the impending dangers lurking in the woods as an early winter storm sets in. Soon the snowy countryside will run red with blood on TERROR MOUNTAIN.

CHECK OUT OTHER GREAT CRYPTID NOVELS

RETURN TO DYATLOV PASS
by J.H. Moncrieff

In 1959, nine Russian students set off on a skiing expedition in the Ural Mountains. Their mutilated bodies were discovered weeks later. Their bizarre and unexplained deaths are one of the most enduring true mysteries of our time. Nearly sixty years later, podcast host Nat McPherson ventures into the same mountains with her team, determined to finally solve the mystery of the Dyatlov Pass incident. Her plans are thwarted on the first night, when two trackers from her group are brutally slaughtered. The team's guide, a superstitious man from a neighboring village, blames the killings on yetis, but no one believes him. As members of Nat's team die one by one, she must figure out if there's a murderer in their midst—or something even worse—before history repeats itself and her group becomes another casualty of the infamous Dead Mountain.

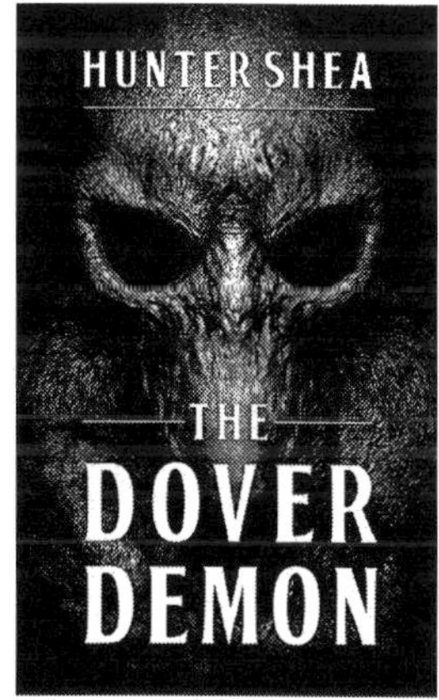

DOVER DEMON
by Hunter Shea

The Dover Demon is real...and it has returned. In 1977, Sam Brogna and his friends came upon a terrifying, alien creature on a deserted country road. What they witnessed was so bizarre, so chilling, they swore their silence. But their lives were changed forever. Decades later, the town of Dover has been hit by a massive blizzard. Sam's son, Nicky, is drawn to search for the infamous cryptid, only to disappear into the bowels of a secret underground lair. The Dover Demon is far deadlier than anyone could have believed. And there are many of them. Can Sam and his reunited friends rescue Nicky and battle a race of creatures so powerful, so sinister, that history itself has been shaped by their secretive presence?

Made in the USA
Middletown, DE
21 May 2020

95581948R00092